the FREE

the FREE

LAUREN McLAUGHLIN

SOHO
TEEN

Published in the United States by Soho Teen an imprint of
Soho Press, Inc.
853 Broadway
New York, NY 10003

Library of Congress Cataloging-in-Publication Data

McLaughlin, Lauren
The Free / Lauren McLaughlin.
ISBN 978-1-61695-731-5
eISBN 978-1-61695-732-2
1. Juvenile delinquency—Fiction. 2. Criminals—Fiction.
3. Family problems—Fiction. 4. Secrets—Fiction.
PZ7.M2238 Fr 2017 DDC [Fic]—dc23 2016020652

Interior art on page 272 courtesy of Georgia Marsh

Interior design by Janine Agro, Soho Press, Inc.

Printed in the United States of America

10 9 8 7 6 5 4 3 2 1

For Jill Grinberg who believed

There is no greater agony than bearing an untold story.
—Zora Neale Hurston

CHAPTER 1

When you're a thief, you're also a liar. It comes with the territory. So I have no problem going along with the cock-and-bull story Mr. Flannery's invented for me. I trust Mr. Flannery. The guy's a genius. If an ex-con can be a genius. He doesn't have a PhD or anything. But he's the best thief I've ever known. And I've known a few. Flannery went down for grand theft auto, did his time, got himself a job as head of the Automotive Department at Donverse Vocational High School. *That* took some genius. The guy convinced people his life of crime was over. Got them to trust him with kids. Genius.

"All you got to do is stick to the story," Mr. Flannery's telling me now, for something like the twelfth time. "Just like we practiced, just like you told the police. You were great in there. Just keep that up. You do that, you do your time. Then we pick up right where left off. Kabeesh?"

We're in Mr. Flannery's office. It's basically a dumping ground of tools, catalogs, and car parts separated from the roar of the auto shop by a dirty glass wall. If you've been invited in there, it's either an honor or the worst day of your life. For me, Isaac West, it's both.

Pat Healy's on the other side of that wall—all six feet, two inches, and three-hundred pounds of him. He's staring at me through that dirty glass with a blowtorch hanging from his fist. Catch Healy in the wrong mood and he's one scary ass white dude. Right now, he looks like he's about to wet his pants.

"Don't you worry about Patrick," Mr. Flannery tells me. "Lord knows *he* ain't talkin'. Guy owes you big after this."

Mr. Flannery's dead right about that. It should be Healy standing in that office, knees shaking, heart thumping, trying to put a brave face on his chickenshit thoughts.

If there was any justice in this world.

Which there isn't.

Anyway, I owe Healy. This will make us square. It was Healy who introduced me to Mr. Flannery in the first place. He vouched for me even though we hadn't seen each other in over a year. Healy is Mr. Flannery's nephew-in-law or third cousin or some kind of distant relative Irish people keep track of.

"Thirty days," Mr. Flannery tells me. "You lucked out there, son. Could have been a lot worse. *Someone's* looking out for you." He winks at me, which turns his freckled face into a mess of wrinkles. "You a praying man, Isaac?"

The answer to that is hell no, but if that's what it takes to get through the next thirty days, I can lie about that too. No problem.

"Juvie's not so bad," he tells me. "I been. Course that was back in the Stone Age. Ask Patrick. He's been in and out a coupla-two-three times. Maybe he'll give you some pointers. He owes you that much. At least."

"Yeah, sure." I keep my answers short because my voice is shaking and I don't want Mr. Flannery to know how scared I am.

I don't want any "pointers" from Patrick Healy, either. After what happened that night, I am not taking Healy's advice on anything.

"Look at me, Isaac," Mr. Flannery says. "You can do this. I wouldn't ask if I didn't believe that. I seen a lot of kids come through here." He looks around the place like he's making sure none of the other students can hear him. Healy, maybe catching on that he's being talked about, looks even more nervous than before. "You remember that first day, when Patrick brought you up here?"

"I remember you making me pee in a cup."

"That's right. Because I don't take druggies into my operation. You into that nonsense, you got no business doing business with me. But I saw something in you. Even that first day. Didn't surprise me in the least when you passed that piss test. You got focus, kid. That's pretty rare in a fifteen-year-old."

"Sixteen," I tell him.

"Shit. When was your birthday?"

"Yesterday."

"Well fuck me. Happy birthday, kid. Wish I had a better present than this."

"It's all right."

Mr. Flannery puts his hand on my shoulder. He's never actually touched me before. "You do this right, you and me got a long and lucrative career ahead of us. I am a loyal man. I do not forget the people who help me."

I'm no brown nose or anything but I have to admit it bigs me up knowing that Mr. Flannery is counting on me to do the right thing here. Before him, I was strictly small time. DVDs, cigarettes, beer—the kind of piddly crap I could steal and resell to the scumbags passing through my apartment. I'd bring down a few extra bucks a week boosting that stuff, then squirrel it away in this rag doll under my sister's bed. Chump change. Especially compared to what I'm earning now with Mr. Flannery. And what I'll be earning again soon. After this little hiccup.

So sure, I'm squared away about taking the rap for Pat Healy. If you're going to think big, you have to take some risks. But, truth be told, I'm not doing it for Healy or Mr. Flannery. I have someone else in mind. And for her there's nothing I wouldn't do.

Not one goddamn thing.

CHAPTER 2

"Lights out, people!"

Reggio, the guard on night watch, a barrel-chested Italian with skinny legs. While he walks the length of the unit, I force myself to yawn. I'm hoping it'll trick my brain into thinking I'm tired. That way, when Reggio kills the lights, I won't have to lie awake in the dark thinking. There's no reason to think now. I'm in survival mode. It's my second night at Haverland Juvenile Detention. Twenty-eight days to go and I haven't slept a wink.

Reggio slows down as he passes my cell. "Time to put that pen down, Ernest." My name's Isaac, but for some reason Reggio has decided to call me Ernest. Probably on account of that writer, Ernest Hemingway.

Cardo, my cell mate, chuckles into the mirror, some cheap plastic thing he has puttied to the wall. It's so warped you can barely recognize your own face in it. "What are you doing?" he asks. "Rewriting the Bible or something?" Cardo's been trying to pick something out of his teeth with the nail of his pinkie for about five minutes. Whatever it is, it's real comfortable in there.

I answer him with a grunt. I figure that's safer than telling him the truth, which is that every time my felt-tip pen touches that notebook, my mind sets off on these crazy journeys. Not like I'm any kind of a writer or anything. Sometimes I'll start one story, then, by the time I get to the end, I'll be telling a completely different one. I don't bother with spelling, and my grammar's all over the place. Once, in middle school, a teacher asked me if English was my first language, probably on account of my being mixed race and looking sort of Cuban. I get that a lot. But English is my first language, and I speak it just fine.

I'm supposed to be writing my "crime story." That's the assignment from my counselor, a spiky little Cubana named *Ms.* Jomolca. Don't call her *Miss* Jomolca whatever you do though because "a woman's marital status is her own business." I learned that on my first day here. I'll call her Queen of the Galaxy if that's what she wants, but no way in hell am I writing down my crime story. That is the one story I cannot tell. And even though I have Mr. Flannery's version memorized and can say it out loud without notes, I figure the less said the better. Bad liars always screw up by piling on the BS, like they can razzle-dazzle you with details. Good liars know that silence is golden because it makes the other guy do all the wondering. Besides, I have plenty of other stories to tell. It's not like my life before juvie was boring. I can write about all the stuff I *didn't* get busted for, like the time I stole that teacher's watch right off her desk when she wasn't looking. That was a sweet take. Lady totally had it coming.

Cardo rips open the Velcro on his sneakers. They're a gift from juvie—stiff white clunkers that make you feel like you've been dipped in concrete. They don't have laces so you can't use them to strangle anyone. The guard who explained this to me at intake actually thought this detail would make me feel safer. At night the sound of Velcro ripples down the unit, and all I can think about is all those necks being saved. For now.

Cardo hops up to the top bunk. A second later, his face pokes over the edge of the mattress. "You get your team assignment yet?"

"What team?"

Cardo coughs out this chimplike laugh, which he does practically every time I speak. "'Coz I hear Barbie Santiago's been reassigned. Again."

"Should I know who Barbie Santiago is?"

Cardo laughs again then rolls back up to his bunk. My ignorance about everything in juvie is already his favorite subject.

I haven't seen any of the girls at Haverland yet. Their cells are in a different wing. But I've overheard the name Barbie Santiago once or twice. Rumor has it her stint in solitary came after a savage beatdown of some girl in her math class who insulted her cousin. Latinas are real big on their cousins. According to the guys I overheard talking about it, Barbie Santiago has a reputation for "fighting like a girl," which is not an insult, by the way. Guys fight for show. Girls fight to kill.

"She a good actress or something?" I ask the springs of Cardo's bunk.

Cardo's face appears over the edge again. Something about his expression reminds me of a monkey, but I keep that observation to myself.

"'Coz I hear there's, like, acting and stuff?" I say. I actually know nothing about nothing, but I've overheard some guys talking about role-plays.

"Yeah, homes. There's acting. But Barbie? She only ever plays the perp. And she real good at it too. She got them Golden Globes locked up, plus an Oscar on the side."

"Awesome."

Too late, I realize that may have come off as sarcastic,

which is not the vibe I want to set with Cardo. I'm aiming for cool. I want Cardo to think I'm the kind of guy who doesn't want any trouble but I'm not about to take any crap either. It's a tough balance and, if I'm honest, I don't always get it right. But Cardo doesn't seem to notice. Or care. He's wrapped up in his own game. Whatever that is.

"And don't think about lying in there either," he says. "Especially if you get Barbie. Girl got some kind of ESP, no'm saying?"

"Yeah, sure."

"*Yeah sure.* Like you already know everything. You don't know nothin' homes."

I'm not about to argue with that. When it comes to juvie, I am greener than snot, which is fine by me. The last thing I want to be is an expert on this hellhole. Get in. Get out. Get back to GTA. That's my game. I have big plans for the money I'll be making with Mr. Flannery, and they do not include playing Mr. Big Shot in a ten-foot-by-six-foot cell for the sake of some Latin gangbanger.

"Good night, ladies!"

Reggio again. He's finished his sweep of the unit, so he kills the lights. There's an eruption of shuffling, some whispers, a few shouts of "Shut up!" Then, once the unit settles, it's dead quiet. Supposedly, Haverland's "special." That's what that judge said, like it was a privilege to get sentenced here instead of some other juvie center. But outside my cell all the local gangs are represented: Bank Street, Sol Dominicano, the Disciples of Vice. I don't see what's so "special" about them, except that they're the worst kids from every school I've ever gone to or been kicked out of. No way am I starting any trouble with these guys. But trouble has a way of finding me. You could say trouble has an unholy crush on Isaac West.

Cardo's face hangs down from the edge of the bunk, a

wisp of a starter mustache catching the red light from something outside our cell. An exit sign maybe. "So, there any blood in your scene?" he whispers.

By "scene," I assume he's talking about my crime story, the one thing I do not want to talk about. With anyone. But I don't want to get on Cardo's bad side by telling him to mind his own business, either. For one thing, Cardo is the only inmate who's spoken to me so far. For another, he's a member of the Disciples of Vice, which is something I put together myself from the Disciples tattoo on his stomach—a smoking joint with a halo around it—because I'm quick like that.

"Yeah," I whisper back. "There's a bit of blood."

"Whatever," he says. "Save it for your team."

I still don't know what he means by team.

CHAPTER 3

The basement cafeteria has slits for windows that are too high to see through and bars on the outside that keep most of the sunlight out. Harsh fluorescents make up the difference, which turns everyone slightly green. Still, all the inmates have figured out how to sort themselves by color, just like they've done in every school cafeteria I've ever been to. This always complicates things for me. Black guys can never figure out if I'm really black. White kids usually think I'm Hispanic. And the Hispanics know I'm not one of them because I don't speak any Spanish, except for some swear words I picked up at this foster home one summer. There's never a separate table for mixed-race kids or for kids who just want to be left the hell alone.

It's the black guys looking at me hardest though, like they assume they're going to end up with me and they're not sure how they feel about it. I know exactly how I feel about it. I don't want to end up with any of these psychos. If I could surround myself with barbed wire I would.

The kitchen adds to the festive atmosphere by serving up their version of fettuccine Alfredo, which makes the whole place smell like feet. I'm standing by the water glasses with my tray, searching for an empty space where no one will notice me, when Cardo waves me over to his table. I don't know what he's thinking. Neither do his friends, each and every one of them a Disciple of Vice. I know charming these monsters is out of the question. But Cardo keeps waving at me, and I don't want to piss off the guy who sleeps three feet above me every night. So I head over with my reeking tray.

"My man," Cardo says.

Silence from his friends, with a side of cold hatred. The table's crowded, no space on the ends, the guys shoulder to shoulder. I stand there like an idiot waiting for someone to make room for me. Cardo just looks at me, like he's waiting for me to figure this one out on my own, like it's a test or something. On the table itself, there's a small space between two trays, so I turn my tray sideways and put it down there, hoping the two guys they belong to will get the hint and make room for me. But one of them, this tall guy with small, piggish eyes, is on his feet in a second.

"The fuck you doing?" he spits at me. "You touchin' me, maricón? You want some of this?"

Behind him, Cardo's eyes are slits. He's watching me, watching his buddy, waiting to see how this ends, like it's a show. A show he started.

"Yo, man," I say, trying to keep it quiet, low key. "I got no problem sitting somewhere else. Too crowded at this table anyway."

"You got a problem with my table now? You saying there's too many of us here? Too many spics for your liking?"

Cardo laughs quietly. Then he pretends to hide that he's laughing. But his friend catches it, turns on him like a viper. "The hell you thinking, bringing this maricón here?"

"Chill, Flavs," Cardo says. "I'm just fucking around. You know me."

"Just fucking around, yeah? How about this?" Without

even turning around to face me, the guy shoots his elbow straight into my gut.

I bend forward out of instinct, but I don't want to make a big deal out of it, so before I hit the floor, I start backing away.

"The hell you think you're going?" the guy says.

"I'm good," I say. "I'm all set, really." I don't know what the hell is coming out of my mouth or where I'm going. I don't even have my tray anymore. I figure I'll just wander around the cafeteria empty-handed. Who needs lunch anyway? I already ate breakfast. That's fine. Hell, I'll skip dinner too. One meal a day. No problem.

"Did I say I was finished with you?" the guy asks.

When I don't answer, he grabs my tray off the table and steps right up to me, jams the tray into my gut, which is still sore. "What's the matter? You don't like sitting with the Disciples no more? You think you're too good for us? Little mayate. Little punk. You hungry? You want your lunch now, you little pussy?"

I keep backing away, inch by inch, but he stays on me, then grabs the tray from the bottom and smashes it all over my scrubs. One swift push and I'm on my ass, covered in shit.

"The fuck?" some kid at a nearby table says.

White, scrawny, buzz cut, he's got a roll stuffed into his mouth. Some of the sauce from my fettuccine has splattered his arm and he's pissed off about it. He breaks off the roll he's chewing and tries to throw it at me, but his aim is pathetic. It hits the Disciple instead. Right in the face.

Now you do not throw bread at a Disciple of Vice unless you've got a death wish. But I want to kiss the guy's dumb white face, because now the Disciple is on him instead of me—wasting no time, just punching the crap out of him. Two seconds of this and the kid's white buddies are up on their feet, going after the Disciple. I'm still on the floor, so I start crabwalking away, put two tables between me and the shit. If I can make it out on my ass, that's fine by me. I'll just crabwalk back to my cell.

Cardo and a few others hang back, but it's a rumble now. Fast and vicious, fists and feet flying. I can't see any weapons, but that won't mean much to the kid who started it. That dumbass cracker is at the bottom of a pile of Disciples, and they will not sleep tonight unless they've jackhammered him. I can feel the tension in the room, the ugly energy. It's fear, excitement. Some of the guys want to jump in, settle their own scores, take a shot at the Disciples or this band of white kids, whoever the hell they are. Everyone else just wants to stay clear. I'm in their camp, trying to make myself as small as possible, invisible if I can.

I played this whole thing wrong. I've got to be smarter. Got to learn how to act here or I'll end up like that cracker. If things had gone differently, if he didn't have the worst fucking aim in the universe, that could have been me down there smearing the floor with blood.

The guards are there all at once, at least eight in total. Batons out, tasers at the ready. They have the table surrounded. When they start peeling the top layer of Disciples off it's like a magic spell. The Disciples put their hands up, let the guards take them away. Heads down, limp. It's like they know the drill, know exactly how much damage they can get away with. I guess it makes sense though. You beat up a kid, that's one thing. You hit a guard, that's another. The guards leave the white kid bleeding on the floor for a while so everyone can have a good look at him. He's not moving, but his stomach's going up and down, which means at least he's breathing. The guards come back in with a stretcher, scrape the kid onto it, and take him away too.

"You take a hit?" one of the guards says to me. "You need to be seen?"

I take my time getting up, make sure I don't draw attention to the pain in my stomach, even though it's screaming. "Naw, I'm good," I say.

Around the cafeteria it's like nothing's even happened. Just another day at lunch.

Cardo motions with his head for me to come over and join him. "There's plenty of room now, ese. Thanks for clearing some space for us. Used to be all crowded and shit." He sticks out his elbows as he digs into his pile of fettuccine. "Come on, man," he says. "You ain't want to be standing there on your own, waiting for somebody else to beat your ass."

Most people don't even see me. But a few do. And they're taking note, making judgments, wondering who the hell I am, being at the center of a rumble. I don't know what kind of impression I've just made. Pussy, I'm guessing. That can't be great. Cardo and the dregs of his crew aren't my idea of great lunchtime company, but it's not like I have other options.

"Come on," Cardo says. "You can have my dessert. Shit's disgusting."

I sit on the corner, across from Cardo, as far away from the other guy on my bench as possible. The other guys start arguing with each other in Spanish. I can't follow much of it, except the part about somebody being "too hot." I assume they're talking about the guy who picked the fight with me. Flavio's his name. Flavio Pendon. I don't want them to know I'm eavesdropping, so I get busy with Cardo's dessert, some kind of green Jell-O with chunks in it, something hard and salty. It might actually be Chex Mix, which makes no sense at all. Cardo's friends keep shooting me evil looks, so I keep my eyes on the next table over. It's one of the few mixed tables in the cafeteria. A tall, stringy Asian kid holds court with a mixed back of whites, Asians, a few Mexicans, and a black dude.

"That's the geek squad," Cardo says. "You sign up for computer class or something?"

I laugh at this ridiculous suggestion. I haven't signed up for anything. When it comes to school, I am a bare minimum kind of guy.

"Well that's the computer class," Cardo explains. "Case you change your mind. So anyway, looks like you'll be getting a new cell mate soon. That's what I wanted to tell you. Wanted to break the news to you face to face. Don't be crying or nothing though."

"You're getting out?"

"Got my court date. This Friday."

The kid sitting next to him snorts. He looks older. He's got a curved scar on his cheek that looks like it's been hardening for years.

But Cardo is only too happy to get a rise out of him. "You see, Isaac." He puts his arm around the guy's shoulder. "Mis amigos don't understand how I could leave all this behind. They be down with the Disciples. They love they barrios. That shit be like *family* to them. But I don't need that family no more. I got me a real family now. I got a woman on the outside and a baby girl on the way. No lo necesito mi barrio. Mi barrio can besa my ass. Shit, I'm moving to Miami when I get out of here."

Everyone goes quiet for a second. Then the kid with the scar offers up something in Spanish, and I don't have to speak the language to know it's a threat.

"Mig, my man," Cardo says. "I didn't see you in there catching Flavio's back. Or any of you guys either." He casts an accusing glance at the other two Disciples.

"Flavio's too hot," Mig says. "I'll be taking that up with him later. But you don't be sitting with the Disciples if you disrespecting us."

"Yo, I ain't disrespecting nobody," Cardo says. "You know I got nothing but 'preciation for the Disciples and what they done for me. But there ain't no Disciples in Miami, no'm saying? And I ain't down with nobody else. 'Sides, I'm tired of this shit. Banging and pumping. Shit's too hard. My woman got an uncle down there who's setting me up. Got a pressure cleaning business, gonna teach me the ropes. Look out, man, I'll be running the show in no time."

Mig laughs.

"What?" Cardo says. "You don't believe me?"

"You think that judge gonna let you out early 'coz of that role-play shit you do? 'Coz your *program?*"

"I'm telling you, man, I been working it. Passed my drug test too."

Mig smushes his lips together in a way only Latinos ever do. "Ain't gonna happen, ese. Early release is for snowflakes and pussies. Spics like us they like to keep around."

"Or send to Walpers," another guy adds.

Walpers is the adult penitentiary where a lot of these guys will end up. Rumor has it the Disciples basically run the place.

"No way," Cardo says. "I ain't being tried as no adult. Lawyer says I got that shit locked down. Only one judge in town got a hard on for that and he ain't sittin' on my case. I'm telling you, I got a good feeling about this one. I been working my program, living clean, staying out of shit in here. You'll see. I'll be enjoying the delights of my woman on the beach in Miami while you be wearing out your wrists in here." He turns to me now. "Ain't that right, cuz?"

Cuz is a dangerous word. I knew a kid once, some wannabe banger, who lost his life over it. You call the wrong guy *cuz,* you could be starting a war you don't even know about. And if someone calls you *cuz,* could be he's saying he likes you. Could be he's marking you out.

"Sure, Cardo," I say. "I hope it all works out just like you got planned."

CHAPTER 4

Later that day I finally learn what Cardo meant by "team assignment." I'm a few minutes early. No way am I blowing it in juvie by showing up late to anything. Whoever's in charge here, you can't give them any reason to mess you up, because in my experience they will take you up on it. There are no windows in the room, and no desks either, just six white plastic folding chairs arranged in a circle. The rug is this sick orange that makes the room feel even stuffier, like it's made of fire. In the corner there's a dented cardboard box with three foam baseball bats sticking out of it.

"You must be Isaac."

This tall, lanky black guy holds out his hand. I can't tell how old he is—north of thirty, south of sixty.

"Yes sir," I say, shaking his hand.

"You're not in the army, Isaac. You don't have to call me sir. My name's Dr. Horton. Have you read the rules of engagement?"

"Um . . ."

He puts his brown leather briefcase on a chair to open it. "For such a bureaucratic institution, these people have no feel for paperwork. Here." He hands me a photocopy with a list of rules on it. First up: *Be Rigorously Honest.*

"Memorize it later," he tells me. "Today, we're just

going to have you listen. We're doing Sandra's crime story. You know what a crime story is, right? You have yours written out?"

"I'm still working on it."

"All right, well don't take too much time. You see, how it works is you read us your crime story, then we role-play it."

He turns and waves to a white girl who's just come in. She's around sixteen with stringy hair the color of dust. Without even glancing at me, she sits in one of the chairs and clutches her notebook to her chest. Her fingers have been nibbled down to nubs.

Two guys come in next, one black with short dreads, one Hispanic. The black guy gives me a head bob. Not hostile but not friendly either. The Hispanic guy comes over and introduces himself as Javier, shakes my hand, then sits down, real professional-like. I take a seat as far away from them as possible.

Next to arrive is this smoking hot Latina with orange-blond hair and thick black roots. "We got new blood in here?" she says. "Nobody told me 'bout this." She sits next to the white girl, tips her chair back on two legs, and sizes me up like I'm a dish of pudding in the dessert line. She is one deadly package. All curves and angles that meet up in ways that are just confusing. But when she smiles this dirty crooked half smile, I catch the one ugly thing about her—a gold tooth front and center. So she's a big-time drug dealer or the girlfriend of one. Good for her.

A white kid enters next, chubby, with an auburn Jew-fro. He notices me but he doesn't say anything.

Dr. Horton puts his briefcase under one of the chairs and joins us in the circle. "This is Isaac West, everyone. Please say hello."

All together they say, "Hello, Isaac." The voice of the

smoking hot Latina is louder than the rest. The girl likes to make her presence known.

"We're going to role-play Sandra's crime story today," Dr. Horton says. "But first I want to introduce everyone to our new team member, so let's go around the room. Tell him your name and . . ." He stops to think for a second. "Your favorite animal." He turns to his left, where the Jew-fro kid sits.

"Hi, Isaac. I'm Riley and my favorite animal is the crebain."

"The fuck's a crebain?" the smoking hot Latina spits out.

Riley doesn't flinch. "They're like these giant crows from Middle-earth. Saruman uses them as spies."

"You talking that *Lord of the Rings* shit again?" she asks.

"No one said they had to be real."

"No, yeah. It's just I was gonna choose that too."

Dr. Horton allows everyone to chuckle at this, then he turns to the black guy with dreads.

"Hi, Isaac. My name's Wayne and my favorite animal is . . ." His eyes shoot up to the low ceiling. "The rat, 'coz it knows how to survive on the street." He turns to the Hispanic guy on his left.

"Hi, Isaac. I'm Javier and my favorite animal is the coyote because it always be outrunning that dude on YouTube."

"You mean the Road Runner," Wayne says. "Coyote's the fool with a anvil fallin' on his head."

Javier shrugs. "That's what I meant. I meant the Road Runner. He one speedy MF."

"That he is," Dr. Horton says. He turns to the smoking hot Latina.

She takes her time, shifts in her seat. When she adjusts the bottom of her red scrub shirt, I catch a flash of creamy beige stomach and the blue ink of a tattoo. It might be a sun, which would put her in Sol Dominicano. Or it might be an upside-down crown, which could mean anything.

"Hi Isaac," she says. "My name's Barbie Santiago, and my favorite animal is the ponketo I iced to get in here. 'Coz he dead now."

So this is the famous Barbie Santiago. It takes no imagination at all to picture her beating down another girl. She has trouble written all over her. The kind of trouble that likes to spread itself around, invite folks in, make them feel at home. I remember reading in one of the helpful pamphlets *Ms.* Jomolca gave me at intake that inmates at Haverland are prohibited from "fraternizing" or engaging in any "romantic or physical relationships" with each other. I figure that type of thing must go on, but I for one do not need some pamphlet telling me to keep my hands to myself. There is no part of Isaac West that is getting near any part of these girls. They're as damaged as goods can get.

"Thank you, Barbie," Dr. Horton says. Then he turns to the stringy-haired white girl.

"Hi, Isaac," she mutters. "I'm-Sandra-my-favorite-animal-is-the-cat-no-reason."

"Well done, Sandra," Dr. Horton says. "Okay, so now—"

"Wait a minute," Barbie says. "What about Isaac? Don't he got a favorite animal?"

"Isaac's going to be listening today. We start slow, remember?"

"Oh yeah. I remember my first time. You never forget your first time."

Wayne rolls his eyes.

"Sandra?" Dr. Horton says. "Are you ready?"

"Not really. Doesn't matter, though, does it?"

"We're all here to support you, Sandra."

"That's right," Wayne says.

"We got your back," Javier adds.

"It's true, Sandra," Riley says. "We're in this together now."

The weird thing is, they aren't even being sarcastic. They actually mean what they're saying. I have never heard anyone talk like that before. No kid has ever had *my* back.

Barbie reaches over and grabs the girl's knee. "It's okay to be scared, Sandra. You be a warrior later. Right now you just give those words to us and we take care of them for you."

Nobody looks less like a warrior than this girl, Sandra. She looks like she's already taken a beating and is just waiting around to die.

For the next few minutes they all discuss who's going to play which part in Sandra's crime story. I stay out of it and read a copy of the notebook pages it's based on. Sandra was hitting a string of convenience stores around Saugus and Revere with this real piece of work named Jared, some twenty-four-year-old scumhole doing double duty as her boyfriend and pimp.

The scam worked like this: Sandra would go in first and pretend she was buying something in the back of the store; then Jared would barge in and stick his gun in the store clerk's face. When Sandra came out from the back and acted all surprised, Jared would grab her, put the gun to her head and tell the store clerk to give him the money or he'd shoot her. They hit about six stores this way, basically playing on people's concern for Sandra. It was a decent scam. There's something so pathetic about Sandra. She's like one of those wounded pigeons you see on the sidewalk hobbling around on one foot. You feel sorry for it, you want to help it, but, at the same time, you don't want to get too close.

Wayne and Barbie are arguing about how to "block the scene." Dr. Horton lets them work it out on their own while I help him move the chairs to the side. After a few minutes, they settle the argument and sit down to watch.

Javier plays Jared, Riley plays the store clerk, and Sandra

plays herself. Even before the scene starts she's shaking. She walks across the room, past Riley and pretends to be shopping for something in the store. Then Javier enters, carrying a lime-green water pistol he's gotten from that dented cardboard box.

"Hands in the air, motherfucker!" he says to Riley.

Riley throws his hands up.

Sandra walks over and pretends to be shocked by what she's seeing. She's a terrible actress. I hope, for her sake, she was more convincing in real life.

Javier grabs her by the head, probably much more gently than Jared ever did. I figure Jared would have had to be rough with her, just to be convincing. But also just to be a dick. I don't know the guy but I know the type. They get a charge out of what they can get over on girls, like it makes them bigger somehow. Sandra pretends to resist, but not that hard. If she was this bad at acting out in the free, no wonder she got busted.

"Give me all the money or I shoot this girl," Javier says. He's a *great* actor. He turns on this cruel streak like he can't wait to shoot Sandra and is secretly hoping the store clerk will make him do it.

Riley pretends to reach into the cash register and hand Javier the money. Javier stuffs the invisible cash in his pants then backs away with that plastic gun at Sandra's head. "Try anything and I shoot this girl."

I haven't read any farther into the story. I figure they must have got caught somewhere down the road, maybe on account of the surveillance cameras or something. But that's not how it went down at all.

When Javier and Sandra put their backs to Riley, Riley pulls out a pink water pistol from the waistband of his red scrubs and points it at Javier's legs.

"Bang!" he says.

Javier hits the orange rug like he's been shot in the back of the leg.

I rifle through the photocopy to check what Sandra's written:

Then D'nesh Patel shot Jared in the back of the knee.

Javier drags Sandra down to the floor with him, which sends his gun sliding across the floor. Sandra pulls herself up to her knees, then very slowly stands up to face Riley.

"Are you all right, young lady?" Riley asks in this bad Indian accent.

Sandra just stands there, staring at him. She looks scared for real now, not like she's acting.

"Get the gun," Javier says. He winces in pain and grabs his knee. "Do it, Sandra. Pick up the goddamn gun!"

This doesn't make any sense to me. But I check the photocopy, and, yes, that's exactly how it went down. Jared used Sandra's real name and told her to pick up the gun.

"Young lady?" Riley says. "Are you all right?"

Then Sandra does the dumbest thing ever. She actually bends down and picks up the gun. What amateurs. Didn't they realize the gig was up at this point? Sandra looks at the gun in her hands, then points it at Riley.

Riley, as the store clerk, looks totally shocked by this turn of events. Who can blame him. I'm shocked too. That store clerk went to the trouble of trying to save Sandra from an armed robber and now she's turning a gun on him? What must he have been thinking? What were Sandra and Jared thinking?

"Do it," Javier hisses.

But Sandra doesn't move. She keeps that gun pointed at Riley's chest.

"I said do it!" Javier yells.

Something's wrong. I can tell from the way Wayne and Barbie are looking at each other.

"Come on, Sandra," Wayne says. "All you got to do is squeeze."

Next to him, Barbie watches the scene more coldly, her right ankle resting on her left knee, man-style. "Aw, come on, Sandra, you want Jared to punch you again? Like he did that time you were pregnant? Who cares about this guy anyway? Some stupid immigrant, probably don't even speak English? Shoot the mother. You know you don't have no choice. You know that pimp of yours gonna beat your ass you don't do it."

But Sandra won't pull the trigger. Instead she closes her eyes.

"Stay with us," Dr. Horton says. He scoots forward on his chair. "Stay with the scene. What happens next?"

"I can't do it."

"Oh, come on," Barbie says. "You know you can do it. You already done it."

Javier, still lying on the floor all twisted up, winces in pretend agony. "Just do it, Sandra, or you know I'll beat your ass."

"No!" Sandra opens her eyes and looks at Dr. Horton. "No, he didn't say that."

Javier slips out of character to apologize, then clenches his teeth and gets right back into it. "Do it," he says. "Just *do* it."

Sandra looks down at Javier writhing on the floor. He's totally helpless, and *still* he has her under his spell. How do guys like that manage it? According to the photocopy, it was Jared who turned Sandra onto both hooking *and* robbery. She was "mostly clean" before that. Lonely and screwed up, but not a hooker and not a thief. Now, here she is, pointing a gun at some store clerk because Jared told her to, a store clerk she *knew*. This whole thing went down in her own neighborhood.

Drop the gun and run, is what I'm thinking. No way in hell would Isaac West get drawn into shooting some guy because a scumbag like Jared told me to. But I am not Sandra.

She looks dazed. Then the fingers of her right hand squeeze the trigger of that water pistol. Riley, whose eyes have been locked on that gun for the last three minutes, hurls himself back into the wall.

"Stay with us, Sandra," Dr. Horton says.

She's staring up at the white ceiling tiles now.

"Stay in the scene."

"Sandra?" Wayne says.

After a pause, she whispers, "I wasn't even there."

"What do you mean?" Dr. Horton asks.

"I mean I wasn't there." Her eyes are glued to the ceiling tiles, like she's watching that store clerk's soul fly away.

Barbie's chair tips forward onto all four legs. "You telling us you didn't shoot that guy?"

"What's his name?" Dr. Horton says. "We use our victims' names in here."

"Sorry," Barbie says. Then respectfully, "D'nesh Patel. Sandra, are you saying you did *not* shoot D'nesh Patel?"

The sound of her victim's name sends a shockwave through her. She wraps her arms around her stomach, then drops to her knees.

Barbie rushes to the floor and takes Sandra's hand. "Talk it out," she says.

Javier, who's been lying at Sandra's feet, contorted, pissed off, and so convincing as Jared I was starting to hate him for real, sits up suddenly. "We're right here," he says. "Whatever it is, you ain't alone with it."

Wayne joins them on the floor too. Then Riley, who's been sliding slowly down the wall, pretending to die from that bullet wound, shuffles over and sits with them. Together, they form a protective shell around her.

I have no idea what's going on. Thankfully, Dr. Horton waves at me to stay put.

"What are you thinking, Sandra?" he asks. "What are you *feeling*?"

"Scared," Sandra says. "Wicked scared."

"That's good," Barbie tells her. "Feelings are good. Isn't that right, Dr. Horton?"

"Feelings are very good. Can you tell us what you're scared of?"

Sandra squeezes herself and rocks back and forth.

"Is it Jared?" Javier asks. "Are you afraid he'll get out and hurt you?"

"No."

"Is it D'nesh Patel?" Riley asks.

Sandra looks up at his freckled face.

"Speak to him," Dr. Horton says. "Go ahead. Tell him what you're thinking."

"I'm sorry," Sandra whispers. "I'm so sorry, D'nesh Patel."

Riley's nostrils flare as he fights off whatever he's feeling. No way is he offering Sandra forgiveness.

"I'm so sorry," Sandra says. "I wasn't even there."

"What do you mean by that?" Dr. Horton asks. "Are you telling D'nesh Patel it wasn't your fault?"

Sandra's eyes stay locked on Riley's. She wants his forgiveness, but he isn't giving it to her, either as himself or as that store clerk.

"I wasn't really there," she says. "It wasn't really me."

Dr. Horton stands up and starts pacing, running his hands over his short hair.

"Come on, Sandra," Barbie says. "You don't mean that, right? You're not saying—"

"You don't understand," Sandra says.

"So explain it to us," Wayne says.

Dr. Horton turns to watch them but hangs back, like he wants them to work this out on their own.

Sandra looks up to him. "It *was* my fault. I *did* do it. But . . ."

"But what?" Wayne asks.

"It's like when I'm on a date. After the money and whatever I have to do to get the guy started, once he gets going, I just kind of drift off."

"To where?" Javier asks.

"Nowhere. It's like I'm not even there. That's what I'm trying to say. That way I can do anything, or let them do anything to me. It's like I'm not even alive when I get that way. Whatever Jared asks me to do, I can do it. Like when he told me to bring my little neighbor along on a date. She was only nine. I knew it was wrong. I was supposed to be babysitting her. It didn't matter though. Jared asked me. I said no at first, like I always do. But then he asked me again and I just went to that place. I told Meg we were going to a movie. I even made her put on this yellow dress she got for her birthday. Thank God all the guy wanted was for her to watch us. Because I don't think I would have stopped him. It was like I'd already made up my mind."

"Yeah," Barbie says. "'Coz you ain't in control your own mind. Your pimp is."

"Maybe she's *too* in control of it," Javier says.

Barbie's eyes flash. "You saying a girl should be *less* in control her own mind?"

"You got to listen to your heart. That's what I'm saying. The heart don't lie. You listen to your mind, it's all practical and shit. It tells you everything's justified when it ain't."

"Them's defenses," Wayne agrees.

"You can't be doing that though," Javier continues. "Because you harden yourself too much, then you don't be seeing other people as human beings. You be seeing them as objects."

"You objectifying," Wayne agrees.

"No." Sandra shakes her head vigorously. "That's not it. I did *not* see D'nesh Patel as an object. I never did that. This is different."

"Yeah," Barbie says. "It's different for girls."

"Um, Barbie," Riley says, "are you saying you did not objectify Enrique Cabron when you knifed him?"

"No, I did not. Because I did not have to. I wanted that motherfucker dead. But we in Sandra's world now. And in Sandra's world she disappearing because she doesn't have any power, see?" Barbie throws her arms around Sandra, tumbling the much smaller girl into an affectionate head-lock. "She got that pimp up in her head telling her what to do, telling her who to be. She been programmed, see? That scumbag broke her down so he could build her up again, the way *he* wants."

"That sounds like guilt avoidance to me," Riley says.

"You think this cracker living without guilt?" Barbie releases Sandra's head from the crook of her elbow. "You guilty, Sandra?"

Sandra nods.

"Then you know what you got to do," Javier says. "You got to stop disappearing. You got to stay here." He drives his pointer finger into the orange rug. "You got to stay present."

"Yeah, Sandra," Riley says. "You have to stop going to that place."

"That place a trap," Wayne agrees.

But Sandra is unconvinced. Her head flops forward in

exactly the same way that Riley's did when he slid down that wall. Barbie inches forward on her kneecaps, then runs her fingers through the girl's dust-colored hair. "You need that place, don't you?"

Sandra nods but won't look up. "I don't know how to live without it."

"You ain't living now," Barbie tells her.

"No, she's living," Wayne says. "It's D'nesh Patel ain't living no more."

CHAPTER 5

Wednesday and Saturday are visitors' days, but I'm not expecting anyone. I know Mr. Flannery can't risk being seen here and I don't have any friends to speak of. That's what happens when you move around a lot. So when a guard meets me after English class the next day to take me to the visitors' room, I'm expecting trouble: the cops coming to question me about my story or, worse, my lawyer with bad news about my sentencing. I still don't understand it. Something about a "defendant capped plea," whatever that means.

The visitors' room is freezing. I spot one dusty radiator in the whole place, but even it looks cold. The guard sits me at the corner of a table and tells me to wait. A white guy from my math class sits at the opposite corner. About fifteen other male inmates sit at the other tables. Nobody speaks to anyone. A few guys rub their arms because of the cold while trying not to look like pussies about it.

A buzzer sounds, a gate somewhere opens, and the visitors start streaming in—mothers mostly, but some girlfriends and children too. My knee bounces under the table. I wonder who it'll be. Then I see her.

"I know I wasn't supposed to come," she says. "But you haven't called."

It's my kid sister, Janelle, her face bursting with those big square teeth.

"Mom's phone number's dead," I tell her. "Come here."

Janelle throws her arms around me. She's wearing my old blue parka. I outgrew it last year. Her dark hair is pulled back neatly in a twist of some kind, straightened, clean-looking. Janelle's three years younger than me, but everyone says we look like twins.

She pulls away and looks up at me. "I guess Mom forgot to pay the phone bill," she says. "Again."

"When has she ever paid the phone bill?"

Best I can tell, our mother has never paid *any* bill.

"Is it okay in here?" She looks around. "Is it safe?"

"Don't worry about me. I got this. I'm learning the ropes."

"And you're still getting out in twenty-five days?"

"Twenty-five days and I'm back in the free. Can you hold on till then?"

Janelle sighs, then sits me down with her at the corner of the bench.

"What is it?" I ask.

"I've been sneaking out."

"Janelle!"

"She made me quit volleyball. She won't even let me go to the library. I have to come straight home after school and just sit there. All day. She says it's because she doesn't want me walking home alone after dark, but you know that's not it."

"Is she—"

"Yeah, she's drinking. She's drinking like crazy. She was drinking before you left. You know that."

Our mother cycles through a range of drinking phases— from buzzed every night to drunk most of the day to falling-down drunk and belligerent to passed out most of the time. She's in the drunk and belligerent phase now, which is her most dangerous.

"So I've been doing what she says. I come home. I go straight to my room. But there's no way I can just sit there all day, Isaac. You know I can't do that."

My sister and I have a strict policy of staying away from home as much as possible, wherever "home" happens to be. I know that sounds like two kids looking for trouble, but actually it's the opposite. Home is where the trouble is. Janelle always signs up for some after-school activity, like volleyball or drama. And I can usually get a job someplace where they'll skip the references thing in exchange for paying me under the table less than the minimum wage. Usually our mother is so wasted she doesn't even know what we're up to, but every once in a while she'll go nuts and make us quit everything so we can be with her all day. She hates being alone.

"Okay, and please don't be mad, but I had to steal some milk crates from Richdales."

"Janelle!"

"My bedroom window's on the second floor. What do you want me to do? Break my leg? It's not really stealing anyway. They're not worth anything."

"Did anyone see you take them?"

"No. They were out back by the dumpsters. They probably don't even realize they're gone."

"No, they realize it. Believe me."

I worked at that Richdales once. They know where everything is. Stealing from them is next to impossible.

But not impossible.

"Mom hasn't seen you?"

"She doesn't see anything. I sneak out. I sneak back in. I'm out for school in the morning before she wakes up. I could be dead for all she knows."

"Where do you go?"

"Mostly I just hang out with Daniela. You'd like her. I think her brother might be in a gang though."

"Janelle, please tell me—"

"Don't worry, I don't have anything to do with *him*. He's, like, seventeen. Hey, by the way, that priest came over. You know the one from St. Joan's? Luckily Mom was passed out. I told him we had to wait. I didn't tell him why though."

"You don't have to wait for me."

"Um, yeah I do. Because if I get baptized and you don't, that means I go to heaven without you."

"It's not about going to heaven, Janelle."

"I know." She looks down and studies her sparkly purple nail polish. It's girlish but still a bit dark for my taste. She's at that crossover age, still a kid in a lot of ways, but boys will be noticing her now. She has to be careful.

"Janelle."

"Oh come on, Isaac, you know I don't want to go to Catholic boarding school. Not without you. We can't afford that anyway."

"You never know."

She looks up from her fingers and studies me.

Janelle knows I'm a thief. I steal things for her sometimes. Clothes mostly. I can't stand seeing her in those charity rags our Mom drags home. And I can get in and out of anyplace with a full backpack in under three minutes as long as the manager's not on the floor. Janelle always tells me, "Isaac, you shouldn't *do* this." But she wears the clothes. Some things you just have to let slide. No matter how wrong they are, you don't go exploring them.

But Janelle doesn't know about my deal with Mr. Flannery. As far as she knows, I'm in juvie for "being in the wrong place at the wrong time." That's what I told her and she sort of believes it. Wants to, anyway. She has no idea I'm going straight back to GTA once I'm out of Haverland. She wouldn't like that at all.

And there's one other thing Janelle doesn't know: I've already gotten her accepted at Holy Name Girls Academy.

I sent in the application myself. I had to forge her signature, but I used her own essay. It was one she wrote for school about dreaming. She won an award for it. The Holy Name people liked it so much they even offered her a scholarship. It won't cover the whole cost, but it'll cover a lot. And I figure between what I have saved up in that doll under her bed and what Flannery tells me I'll be earning between now and next September, I can cover the difference. I'll miss Janelle like crazy when she moves out. But, man, does it put a smile on my face knowing that next September she'll be living in those redbrick dormitories at Holy Name Girls Academy rather than in that rat hole with me and our mom.

"You let me worry about the money," I tell her. "You just keep your head down and your grades up."

Her eyes get small like she's trying to figure out what her brother is up to. That's a dangerous game, though, and she knows it. "Yeah, well, I still think we should both get baptized," she says. "But not Mom."

"Deal." I hold up my fist and she bumps it.

"So hurry up and get out of here," she says.

"That's the plan."

CHAPTER 6

The next day, Dr. Horton surprises me in the orange-rug room by pulling me aside while the others are still straggling in. "I didn't realize how short your sentence is, Isaac. We need to get to work. Have you got your crime story?"

"Are we done with Sandra already?"

Sandra sits alone, hugging her knees against her chest. We spent the whole last session replaying her crime story with different people in different roles. Not me though. I was still in "listening mode." Every time they got to the gunshot, no matter what part Sandra was playing, she'd glaze over. Disappearing, she called it. Like she could take herself out of her own life. I couldn't blame her for trying. If I had Sandra's life, I'd want to disappear too. Her mother's an addict who disappears (literally) for weeks on end. Her father left when she was twelve, after molesting her for a year. Jared the pimp is the closest thing she has to family.

"Sandra needs a break," Dr. Horton says. "We'll get back to her later. What do you think?" His face turns bright, like he's offering me a delicious cookie.

Adults can be so obvious.

"I just have to read it, right? We're not gonna act it out or anything."

"Just reading for today. One step at a time."

"Hey man," Javier says. "It's okay if you're nervous. Everyone gets nervous when they read their crime story."

"Not me," Barbie says. "I've read it twice now. Piece of cake."

"That's because you one frosty bitch," Wayne offers up.

"You got me wrong. You don't know nothing about me."

"That's great, Barbie," Riley says. "But we were talking about Isaac, in case you didn't notice."

Barbie leans back and crosses her ankle over her knee. "I know who we're talking about. I just want Isaac to know it's okay *not* to be nervous too."

Sandra stays out of it and watches everyone from behind her knees.

"Barbie's right," Dr. Horton says. "All we ask for is your honesty."

"Right," I say. "Honesty. Sure."

I sit down, take out my notebook, and flip to the page where my crime story begins. It's the last thing I wrote, and even though I've practiced this a million times with Mr. Flannery, I'm still nervous about it.

"Okay. My crime story began on May twenty-seventh."

"Speak up," Barbie says.

I look up, then start again.

"My crime story began on May twenty-seventh. I was bored one night, so I decided to steal a car. It was a Cadillac Escalade. It was late, around one thirty, and there were no lights on at the guy's house. It was a real quiet street too. I smashed in the window, hot-wired it, and started to drive away. But then the owner came out and he was real drunk. He grabbed the driver's door and opened it. Then he dragged me out and started punching me. So I punched him back once and he fell over and didn't get up. I got back in the car and drove it away. I drove it around for a little while, then I got scared, so I dumped it in Pleasance Pond."

I close the notebook, and when I look up, all five of my teammates plus Dr. Horton are staring at me.

"That's it?" Barbie says.

Wayne chuckles.

"Where was this?" Barbie asks.

I look at Dr. Horton because I was under the impression I only had to *read* my crime story, not discuss it.

"It's all right, Isaac," Dr. Horton says. "You can answer that."

"Um," I say. "It was in Waverly?"

"Is that a question?" Barbie asks. "Are you asking me or telling me? Was it in Waverly?"

"Yeah. It was in Waverly."

"What were you doing in Waverly? You live there? 'coz you don't look like no Waverly kid. Where you go to school? St. James Prep or something? You a rich kid posing as a poor kid? You a narc?"

The others laugh.

"Barbie," Dr. Horton says. "Is any of that constructive?"

"I live in Worthrop" I tell her.

"So how'd you get to Waverly?" Barbie asks. "That's, like, ten miles. At least. Did you drive there? You have a license? What happened to your car?"

"I didn't . . . drive there."

"So how'd you get there?"

"I rode my bike," I say.

I don't even own a bike, never have, but she doesn't know that.

"So what happened to it?" she asks. "Did you go back and get it afterwards? You know, after you dumped that car into a pond?"

Wayne chuckles again.

"Um . . . no . . . I put it in the back of the Escalade."

"Oh," Barbie says. "Because you didn't say nothing 'bout that. Also did you take it out before you dumped that batshit expensive car into a pond?"

"Yes. That's how I got home."

"How'd you get the car into the pond?" Wayne asks. "What'd you do, push it?"

"Yeah."

"By yourself? An Escalade?"

"That's a big car," Barbie says.

"It's a truck actually," Riley adds. "Also, the Escalade has one of the most sophisticated antitheft devices on the market. My uncle has one. How'd you override it?"

Jesus Christ! The cops never asked me any of these questions.

"Are you gonna answer or what?" Barbie asks.

"Hey, Barbie," Javier says. "Take it easy, all right?"

"I'm just trying to get the facts straight. I mean, if we're gonna role-play this, I need to know how it went down. Ain't that right, Wayne?"

"Mmm-hmmm."

"Yeah," Riley says. "You're not giving us much to work with, Isaac. I mean, why did you pick that car? How did you hot-wire it? Where'd you learn to do that?"

"And what about the owner?" Barbie says. "You didn't use his name. We use our victims' names here."

"It's Sal. Sal Christaldi."

"What's that, short for Salvatore?"

"Yeah."

"Okay. So this Salvatore Christaldi comes after you and you drop him with one punch?"

"That don't sound right," Wayne says.

"What are you?" Barbie says. "Five eight? About one thirty?" She gives me a crushing up and down.

"I'm five *nine*." And still growing, I want to add, but I don't.

"Still," she says. "One punch?"

"Yeah. One punch."

"That's one hell of a punch," she says.

"Well there was a rock on the ground."

"Huh? What rock? You didn't say anything about a rock."

"There was a rock. I didn't see it though. I guess he hit his head on it when he fell over."

"You *guess?*" she says.

"It was dark. All's I know is what they told me afterwards. That he hit his head on a rock."

"So what happened to him?" Javier asks. "You said he didn't get up again. He okay now?"

Thank God the cops weren't this nosy. They hardly asked me a thing. There was a rock on the ground. I punched Mr. Christaldi and he fell on it. Boom. Done. I told them this story once, then wrote it down for them and signed my name. No problem. The cops were *nice.* Got me a soda and a bag of chips. Believed every word of that story, or at least didn't care enough to question it. But these guys, Jesus, they're like vultures. Sandra got the same treatment during her role-play. *After* the group hug. The group hug was just a way to soften her up. *What were you thinking the second you picked up that gun? How did you feel in your stomach? In your head? Were you hot? Were you cold?* They stripped the poor girl raw, and now look at her. She's hugging her knees and chomping on her fingers. This is supposed to rehabilitate people?

"Yo, Isaac?" Barbie starts in again. "So what happened to Mr. Salvatore Christaldi? You telling us you killed him with one punch?"

"No, I didn't kill him. He's alive. But . . ."

"But what?"

"He hasn't woken up yet."

They all look at each other.

"When was this?" Wayne asks. "You said May?"

"End of May."

"So he's in a *coma*?" Riley asks.

"And he's just lying there?" Wayne says. "Like a vegetable?"

"No," Riley says. "A coma is when your eyes aren't even open. It's more like being asleep, right?"

Riley looks at me as if I'm an expert in comas, which I am not. Maybe I should be, on account of being at least partly responsible for the state Mr. Christaldi is in. I hate what happened to him. It's horrible. He didn't deserve that. He didn't deserve to have his car stolen either, but whoever said life was fair?

"I hear some of them coma people can actually hear things," Javier says. "They're like awake and stuff, but they can't do nothing. Can't speak. Can't move."

Sandra, who hasn't said a word the whole time, shudders noisily.

"Man," Wayne says. "That's some dark shit."

"Are they gonna pull the plug on him?" Riley asks.

"No way," Javier says. "You can't do that. Guy could be wide awake in there, having whole conversations with himself. Maybe wake up tomorrow or the next day."

"Or never," Riley says. "And in the meantime it costs like a gazillion dollars a day to keep him alive."

"You can't put a price on a human life," says Javier.

"Well you could have," Barbie says. "If Isaac hadn't driven that *Escalade* into a *pond*."

That's the troubling detail for Barbie, the fact that I threw away all that money. The way she's looking at me now, with that crooked half smile and her gold tooth shining, I can't tell if she thinks I'm the dumbest punk in the world, or the worst liar. I'm rooting for dumbest.

There's nothing in the Rules of Engagement about being dumb. Lying, on the other hand, is against Rule Number One. But even if she thinks I'm lying, she has no proof. No one does, except Sal Christaldi.

And he isn't talking.

CHAPTER 7

The next day a guard meets me outside of English class and escorts me to a conference room down the hall that reeks of old coffee. There's a tall guy with a pale, shiny head waiting for me.

"Hi, Isaac," he says.

It takes me a second to recognize my lawyer. I only met him that one time in court and he barely said a word. I can't remember his name. Sloane? Sears? Something with an *S.* I do remember that tie though—yellow with a ketchup stain in the shape of a dog. The fact that he's still wearing it means they must not pay these guys very much.

He slides his briefcase onto the chipped table and opens it. "So Sal Christaldi has woken up."

"What?" I practically choke on the word.

"Got some nerve damage. Possible hearing loss. He's lost a lot of weight too. He's in pretty rough shape actually. On the plus side, he's alive. And he'll probably make something close to a full recovery. Except for the hearing loss."

I do my best to stay calm, try to find my game face. It's not like I wanted Mr. Christaldi to stay in that coma forever. His waking up is great news. For *him.*

"Yeah, the thing is, Isaac, his version of events doesn't quite match up with yours. Apparently he's saying some *giant* attacked him." He gives me a quick up and down. "A *white* giant." He shows me a printout of an email with the words *a giant attacked me* highlighted in lime green. "He also says there was some black kid hiding under a truck. I presume that was you?"

I open my mouth to speak, then decide against it.

"Well, at any rate, the ADA wants this Caucasian giant's name. If you give it to her, she's willing to consider overlooking the fact that you lied in court, which is perjury, by the way. Why did you do it?"

"Um . . ."

"Never mind. It doesn't matter why you did it. Whoever this giant is, he's up for attempted murder, so . . ."

"Attempted *murder*?"

"Yes. And the ADA wants his name." He looks at me like this is the most reasonable request ever, and I'd have to be a total dick not to come up with the goods.

"I can't," I tell him.

"You can't what?"

"I can't give you his name."

"Why?"

"I don't . . . I don't know it."

"You're telling me you don't know the name of the guy who stole that car with you?"

"Yeah."

He stares at me, his clean-shaven white face blank. He should take as good care of his ties as he does his skin. "Okay. Let me see how I can put this. That's an obvious lie, and there's no way Jill Levy is going to believe that."

"Who's Jill Levy?"

"She's the ADA. And she is not joking around, Isaac. She's never liked this case. She thinks there are too many holes in it. But until now she's had nothing to go on. Sal Christaldi changes that. She wants to start filling in those holes."

I look down at my hands, which is exactly what Janelle does when she doesn't want to talk about something. It's a giveaway, a tell. I need to work on that.

"Okay. Isaac, let me explain about perjury. You know what it is, right?"

"Yeah, I know what it is. It's lying."

"Yeah, but it's a special kind of lying that comes with a brand-new sentence." His voices rises, just a little. "So forget about the thirty days. You could get an extra six months for that."

"Six months?"

"Or more."

Finally I look at him. "What if I just met him that night? What if he never told me his name? I mean; why would he?" I'm improvising now, which is dangerous. This is how bad liars get caught. It's why I'm supposed to stick to the script, like Mr. Flannery said.

"How'd you meet him?"

I shrug.

"Isaac, listen to me." He leans forward, and my eyes are drawn back to the ketchup stain on his tie. "It's in your best interest to be honest with me right now. Your story is in shambles. The ADA already knows you lied. And I know Jill Levy. I've dealt with her before. She's an ambitious little . . . well, trust me on this. She will not be persuaded by your youth. If perjury is the only card she has to play, she will play that card. You want to risk another six months? Possibly more?"

When I don't answer, he just stares at me. He's real patient about it too, like he has all day to wait me out. But my lawyer will never win at that game. If anyone has all day to wait, it's the kid serving time.

"I have to make a phone call," I tell him.

"Suit yourself," he says. Then he shoves the papers back in his briefcase and leaves.

CHAPTER 8

At the payphone, there's some lanky white kid with his arm around the box like he's making out with it. I'm next followed by six other guys who are running out of patience. I've got the piece of paper in my hand. It's not Mr. Flannery's actual number. Calling him directly from juvie would be too dangerous. It's an emergency number where I can get a message to him. I'm only supposed to use it in case of an "absolute fucking end of the world emergency." I figure this qualifies.

"Yo, we ain't got all day here."

It's the kid behind me. Scrawny, five foot nothing. Looks about twelve years old, but a hard-living twelve.

The white kid hangs up finally, and I step up to the phone. I'm surprised when a woman answers. She sounds white, middle-aged, with a thick Revere accent.

"Hi, it's Isaac West. I need to get a message to . . ." I'm not sure I'm supposed to say Flannery's name. "Someone?"

"A message to *someone*? Am I supposed to know what that means? What, are you on drugs or something? Aw, wait. Don't tell me. Hold on. Hold on. Barney! Hey Baahney! I think it's someone for that dickhead bruthah of yohz." The phone drops. There's some muffled movement, then someone else picks up, a man this time.

"Who is this? Did he give you this number?"

"Um yeah, I just need to get a message to him."

In the background that lady yells, "You tell that piece-a-shit brothah of yohz to keep that gahbidge outta this house. Ya heeya me?"

"Shut up, Krissy! Okay, look. Don't call here again. I don't care what he told you. Do not call here."

"But I really need to—"

"Do *not* call this number."

Click. Dial tone.

The son of a bitch hangs up on me.

CHAPTER 9

That night I have the cell to myself. Cardo's gone, the lucky bastard, probably on his way to Miami to sample the delights of his girlfriend and learn about pressure cleaning. I'm happy for him. I really am. But I could have used his ear tonight. He's an expert in everything, at least in his own mind. Right or wrong, he would have something to say on my predicament. What would Cardo do? Jesus, when you find yourself asking that question, you know shit's gone down.

When I agreed to take the rap for Healy, I knew it could have been anywhere up to six months. That's what Mr. Flannery told me. I was okay with that too. I owed Healy for getting me onto Flannery's crew. And I knew I was buying a lifetime's worth of loyalty from Mr. Flannery for making the sacrifice. When the thirty-day sentence came down, I felt like the luckiest kid alive. But I've gotten used to the idea now. Thirty days I can live with. Six months seems like forever. Especially with Janelle sneaking out of the house every day. That's not a situation that'll get better with time.

I need to get home. I've got twenty-two days left of my current sentence, and I'm seriously considering dropping a dime on Pat Healy.

AT BREAKFAST THE NEXT day, I'm bleary eyed. I haven't slept. I haven't figured anything out either. I'm standing outside the kitchen like a zombie with my powdered eggs and toast, trying to figure out where to sit. With Cardo gone, I know I won't be welcome at the Disciples' table anymore, not that I particularly liked their company.

"Yo, what you standing there for?"

It's some wormy white kid coming up behind me. I step out of his way and *Bam!* My tray meets with something solid. Not a wall though. A wall would be great news. Instead it's someone's stomach. And not just anyone's stomach either, but the one belonging to Cecil Boone, a three-hundred-pound black tower of hazard and gold teeth. Drug dealer, murderer, and member of the Bank Street gang, Boone is the kind of guy everybody knows. If there's a list of the top five people you should not bump into with your damn breakfast tray, Cecil Boone is numbers one, two, and three.

The collision is minor. I don't actually drop my tray. Nothing breaks or splashes out. Not a speck of food even touches him. But, like a dick, he decides to be a dick about it. He glares at me in a way that is exactly like cocking a gun. And just like that I'm on the goddamn stage again. But I've learned a thing or two since my run-in with Flavio Pendon. The trick is to avoid being *too much* of a pussy about things. Guys like Cecil Boone can smell that kind of fear. And they like it.

"Sorry, man." I keep it quiet, respectful, but not too submissive. My plan is to move on, leave it behind like the minor incident it is.

But Boone is dug in. He's not going anywhere. And it's going to take more than the words "sorry" and "man" to get him past this. The best way out is for someone to come smack me upside the head, call me out for being so clumsy, then reassure Boone that I'm "all right." But who's going to do that? Cardo's gone. Nobody else even knows me.

The whole place starts to hush and the faces staring back all say the same thing: *Whoever the hell you are, don't even* think *about bringing that shit over here.*

So what do I do? The only thing I can think of. I pick out the weakest group in the room and I take the shit to them.

I put my back to Boone (a risky move on its own), then I walk real calm and slow, like this was my plan all along, straight over to the geek table. These guys look at me like I'm the Grim Reaper, which I guess in a way I am. I don't say anything. I just slide in next to this white sliver of a kid who scoots as far away from me as possible until he bumps into the Mexican on his right. At the head of the table that Asian guy with the bushy hair stares at me, bug-eyed. The one black guy scowls. I dig into my eggs like they're the most delicious meal I've ever eaten and pretend like nothing unusual is going on, like I've been sitting there all along and they just haven't noticed me.

Eventually the black guy says, "The hell you think you doin'?" He's tall, broad-shouldered, with short hair and cold eyes that mean business.

"What?" I say. "You guys are the computer class, right? I want to sign up."

The Asian guy with the bushy hair whispers to a redheaded kid with braces.

"I'm Deon," the black guy says. Then he does something that is either stupidly brave or bravely stupid: he reaches across the table and shakes my hand, *in front of everyone,* including Cecil Boone. "Computer class meets every day. Even weekends. You cool with that?"

"Yeah," I lie. "I'm cool with that."

They're all looking past me now. Based on the way their

eyes are moving from left to right, I figure Boone must have had his fill of bullshit for the morning and is on his way. I don't turn around to look though, because that would make me look like a pussy, otherwise known as an invitation to permanent abuse. This time, I've played it right.

"We got email, you know," the thin white kid says.

"Yeah but it's not about that," the Asian guy at the head of the table says. "If you're coming in just for email and porn, you can forget it."

"Yeah," Deon says. "We in there to work."

"And no Facebook," the Asian guy adds.

"That's Stanley Huang, by the way." Deon jerks his head toward the Asian guy. "He and Mr. Klein sort of run the class."

"Wait, so if I sign up, I get an email address?" I ask.

"Don't you have one already?" Huang asks.

"No."

Deon snickers. "You a newbie. Don't worry about it. I was too. Never touched a computer. Now I'm designing the newsletter."

"What newsletter?"

The thin white kid laughs.

"Shut up, Anthony," Deon says. "We got a monthly newsletter. It's called *The Free.* You never read it?"

"I just got here," I tell him.

"Nobody reads the newsletter," Anthony says. "Which is whack because it's good. Deon's gonna be a journalist. Ain't that right, Deon?"

"Yeah, that's right. Soon's I get out of here, get my diploma, I'm gonna be a freelance investigative reporter."

"So I can email anyone I want?" I ask. "Like . . . anyone?"

Deon rolls his eyes. "Yeah, but you got to work first. That's what I'm trying to tell you. It's not just about goofing off. No checking email . . ."

"Till after you've done your work," everyone at the table says at the same time.

"That's rule number one," Stanley Huang adds.

"What's rule number two?"

"No Facebook," they all say.

CHAPTER 10

It's a dim room with dirty shades pulled all the way down and fifteen identical silver laptops bolted to some folding tables. The tables are flimsy and light. It would be nothing to collapse one and make off with six laptops. Not that I'm planning to do that, but a thief's instincts die hard.

There are a few girls in there, but it's mostly guys. The teacher, a young scraggle-haired white guy in a black T-shirt, huddles with Stanley Huang while I wait for someone to teach me something. I have a laptop open in front of me, but Mr. Klein has told me not to touch it yet. Everyone else is busy typing lord knows what. But if they want to talk or laugh about something, that's fine. It's the most laid-back class I've ever been to.

All I want to do is get online and track down Mr. Flannery's email address so we can figure out what to do about Sal Christaldi. But there's a password to get online and I'm supposed to do my "work" first. Whatever that is.

Eventually, Stanley Huang comes over and sits next to me. According to Deon, he's the teacher for "newbies" like me. Mr. Klein spends his time teaching programming to the more advanced students, like Anthony and that redheaded kid named Fitzpatrick, plus one of the girls. Huang is already an advanced programmer. He's been designing his own video games since he was ten. Teaching "the basics" to newbies like me is part of his sentence.

"So you're like completely computer illiterate?" he asks me.

"I'm not *illiterate*. I can read."

Huang sniffs, then types something into my laptop and we're off.

I want to quit a dozen times. I want to smash the laptop twice. Fonts, formatting, margins, toolbars. Word processing can blow me. All I want is to email Mr. Flannery. Through it all, Huang keeps groaning about how "incredibly basic" all of this stuff is, like I must be stupid for not already knowing it.

"I hate this shit," I finally say.

"Chill out," Deon tells me. He's been bashing away at the laptop next to us, making charts and diagrams for his newsletter. "You'll get it. Just takes practice."

"*You* were much faster than this, Deon," Huang tells him.

Huang's a prick. No denying that. Out in the free, he would know his place. But in here he gets to be a little king, with his army of geek worshippers. Big deal. I never wanted to be a king. Too much responsibility.

"What's a template?" I ask the little genius.

Huang rolls his eyes. He's real good at this. He can roll them in both directions. Just one of his many awe-inspiring talents.

SOMEHOW, AFTER BATTLING WITH Huang and the laptop for nearly an hour, I learn how to "format a business letter," a skill I am one hundred percent certain to put to use right away in my new career as a businessman the second I get out of juvie. Huang has more important things to do, so he hooks me up with an email account, then tells me to keep practicing with an online tutorial.

The second he's gone, I go online to look for Mr.

Flannery's email address. I'm not totally computer illiterate. I know a couple of things. I've used my sister's email address a few times at the library. I know about Google. It's not hard to find the website for Donverse Vocational. The auto department has its own page, with a nice photo of Mr. Flannery and the other teachers. He's drinking from that giant red coffee mug he always carries and making that face he always makes, like he's amused by something. I've always liked that about Mr. Flannery. No matter what's happening in the auto shop, he's never surprised. A kid could blow up a car by accident right beside him and Mr. Flannery would just chuckle to himself, like he's seen it all before.

But there's no email address for Tom Flannery. None for any of the auto-shop guys, either. Most of the other teachers have email. The principal has email. There's a special email for "inquiries." But nothing for Tom Flannery.

"Who's Tom Flannery?"

I look up and spot Barbie Santiago hovering over me.

"You go to Donverse?" she asks. "I got a cousin there. Culinary arts. You in the auto program? Oh yeah, of course. You a big-time car thief. Who's that guy?" She points to the photo of Mr. Flannery.

"Are *you* in this class?" I ask her.

"You're late, Barbie," Mr. Klein says.

Quick as a switchblade, Barbie pulls out a small slip of paper from the waistband of her scrubs. That tattoo again on her stomach. It *is* a sun, which means she's Sol Dominicano, a gang that controls most of the crank in the area and is perpetually at war with the Disciples of Vice. The news just keeps getting better with this girl.

"Emergency meeting with my lawyer," she says. "I got wheels turning."

"I see you know Isaac," Mr. Klein says.

"Oh yeah, we go way back." She sidles around to the other side of the table and opens the laptop opposite me. "Hi Marley," she says to one of the girls.

Marley nods cautiously.

The other girls regard Barbie with a spiky combination of fear and contempt, which Barbie absorbs without a hitch. She owns the room now that she's in it, just like she owned the orange-rug room.

"Let's see, where was I?" She starts typing and eventually gets lost in whatever she's doing. But every once in a while she looks up and rests those amber eyes on me, like she knows something, like she can see straight through my lying little heart. Just like Cardo warned me about her.

CHAPTER 11

Later that day, a guard brings me back to the visitors' room and who is waiting for me at one of those tables? None other than Tom Flannery himself. He has his hands stuffed into the pockets of his Carhartt jacket. Head down, eyes dancing around the room, he looks like a caged wolf. His face seems paler than usual, like his freckles have been painted on.

"I called that number," I tell him, "but that guy told me—"

"Yeah, yeah," he interrupts. "I got the message. You doin' okay in here? You holding up?"

"Yeah, I'm all right, but we've got a problem, Mr. Flannery. Sal Christaldi woke up and—"

"I know all about Sal Christaldi," he interrupts again. "It changes nothing."

"But he knows it wasn't me who hit him. He knows it was someone else. A giant, he says. A *white* giant. And now this ADA lady wants me to ID him."

"Have you said anything?" For someone who always seems amused, never surprised, he doesn't look amused now.

"No. But my lawyer says I'm up for perjury if I don't give him up."

"Slater told you that? Did he tell you to give up Patrick?"

"Um . . ."

"Well did he or didn't he?"

"No. He just said . . . Wait, do you know my lawyer?"

"I make it my business to know who's looking after my crew, kid. Now, what did Slater tell you?"

"He said I could be charged with perjury."

"That's bullshit. They can't prove anything."

"But they've got Sal Christaldi. What if he IDs him?"

Mr. Flannery snorts. "Don't worry about Sal Christaldi. He ain't ID-ing anyone."

"How do you know?"

"Because if he could, they wouldn't be asking you for anybody's name."

I have a think about this. It's a good point, actually. Maybe they were just trying to scare me.

"Look, don't worry about the ADA," Mr. Flannery says. "That's nothing but smoke and mirrors. And your lawyer's just dropping the word *perjury* in there to cover his ass, tick off a box, so he doesn't get in trouble with his own people."

"Are you sure? Because he definitely told me I could get another six months. Or more."

"He's exaggerating. Believe me, Slater's looking out for himself more than he's looking out for you. And look, even if you did get more time—"

"So you think I could?"

"Isaac, listen to me. You think I like having you in here? You're my best kid. It broke my friggin' heart sending you here in Patrick's place. That kid . . ." He does that thing where he looks around to make sure no one's listening. "The kid's an idiot. I know he's family and all, but he's an idiot. I only took him under my wing on account of my cousin, which is a long story I don't want to get into. If the kid wasn't already eighteen, believe you me, it would be him in here instead of you."

But with Healy, it would be hard time, in the big house, which is a hell of a lot worse than six months in juvie.

I know. I know. I shouldn't complain. I remember Healy telling me about the time he visited his father in prison. We were sitting in Healy's pickup truck, around the corner from Sal Christaldi's house, waiting to run down the clock so we could get started. Healy got real serious, told me his father was basically a good guy. A low-level street dealer, weed mostly, nothing big. He got busted in a dragnet. Healy went to see him in prison and he looked like hell, skinny, battered, totally paranoid. He told Healy "whatever you do, don't end up here. Prison's not for people like us." Turns out the old man was right too. A few days later he was shivved in the throat, bled out in the toilets before anyone found him.

I remember the way Healy looked when he told me the story, the whites of his eyes screaming out against the dark. I could practically smell the fear coming off of him. "I'm not ending up like that," he said. "I'm never going to jail." Maybe that's why he lost his cool with Sal Christaldi that night. He was thinking about his father, about prison, about how one wrong move—one *witness*—could destroy you.

"Listen to me, kid," Flannery says. "We gotta think strategic. Think long term. 'Coz I thought you were in this for the long haul."

"Yeah, I am. It's just—"

"You got big plans, right? Private school for your sister? That costs money, doesn't it?"

The thought of Janelle sends my heart into my throat.

"I remember that picture you showed me," Flannery goes on. "Shit, if I had a sister that pretty, I'd want her in Catholic school too. Let the nuns look after her. They'll keep her safe. My sister was a dog." He chuckles. "Still is."

I laugh out of respect, but there's no feeling in it.

"We got a good thing going here, Isaac. You and me. A real good thing. But sometimes you gotta take one for the team. I know. I've done it myself a few times."

"Really?"

"Sure. Sure. And it's a real bitch. I know that. You do your best work, keep your head down, keep your nose clean, you follow orders like you're supposed to. And then some a-hole loses his shit and turns a simple boost into an aggravated assault."

"Murder," I whisper. "My lawyer said attempted murder."

"Not for you though."

"No, for me it's just perjury."

"The most candyass rap of all. Look, it's Patrick who should be worried about this development, not you. All you have to do is keep your mouth shut. They can't make you talk. Am I right? What are they gonna do, come in here and torture you until you speak?"

"No. Yeah, you're right."

"So I can count on you?"

I take a deep breath and try to find my resolve, or at least the look of it. "Yeah. Of course you can count on me, Mr. Flannery. I ain't dropping a dime on anybody. I just, you know, I just wanted to make sure you knew about Mr. Christaldi, that's all. See if it changed the plan."

"Oh, right. I see. No, I'm glad you got in touch. Gives me a chance to check up on my favorite student." He throws me a quick wink. "I'd come by more often only I've got appearances to think about. You know how it is."

"Yeah, of course."

"I'm an upstanding member of society." He chuckles. "Look at me, Isaac. You're worried about something. What is it, your sister? You want me to check up on her? Where's she go to school?"

"Worthrop Middle School."

"I know some people there. I can put some eyes on her. You're a good brother. Girl's lucky to have you. I hope she realizes that. No father around. Mother maybe not so reliable."

That's a generous way of putting it.

"You're all she's got," he goes on. "I know how it is. You want to get out of here as soon as possible so you can keep an eye on her. Makes perfect sense. I'll tell you what, if you do get busted for perjury—and believe me, there is no way that's happening—but if you do, I will personally look out for your sister. What's her name again? Jeanette?"

"Janelle."

He nods, glancing toward the door. The color has come back to his cheeks. He's his old carefree self again. "Janelle," he says. "Right. Pretty name. I'll look out for her myself. Heck I'll drive her to and from school if you want. Make sure she gets home safe and sound. How's that?"

"Yeah. Thanks, Mr. Flannery."

I don't tell him that getting home safe and sound isn't the problem. Janelle can do that on her own. It's *being* home that's the problem.

CHAPTER 12

On Monday, my lawyer, Mr. Slater, returns to that conference room with two detectives. They're the same ones who questioned me after the thing with Sal Christaldi.

"We were hoping you could have a look at these," one of them says. He's Hispanic, with a friendly face. He slides an open laptop toward me.

"I told Jill Levy you didn't catch the giant's name," Slater says. "But maybe you'll recognize his face."

"Just use the down arrow to scroll through them," the Hispanic detective says. The other detective, white, older, says nothing. He's expecting me to screw this up somehow.

After a while, the faces start to blend together, one white delinquent after another. Healy's picture is on the fifth page. He looks lost, like he meant to show up for a school photo and wound up getting a mug shot instead.

Healy's a mixed bag. I met him two years ago at this rancid shelter in Revere, one of the worst hellholes I've ever called home, and there is some stiff competition for that title. He was running with a gang of losers who called themselves "the Revered." Nobody else called them that. They were small time, mostly hung around the stairwells drinking, smoking pot, sold a dime bag here and there. I figured the best way to keep them off my back was to throw them a pack of cigarettes every now and then, which actually worked. That's how lame they were. Banger wannabes.

When my mom moved us from Revere to Worthrop, I forgot all about Patrick Healy. He didn't make much of an impression on me and I would have thought it was vice versa. But then I got expelled from Worthrop High over an incident between my fist and some white kid's nose. I wound up at Donverse Voke and Healy went out of his way to take me under his wing there. It was like he had a completely different memory of our time at that shelter, like we were good friends or something. I figured it was all the pot he smoked. Or maybe he had me confused with another kid in that gang. There was this young kid who looked a little bit like me.

Whatever the reason, Healy was all about showing me the lay of the land at Donverse. It was basically reject central unless you were in the auto program. And the auto program was reject central unless you were on Mr. Flannery's crew. Healy was a serious student of the automotive arts by then. He was out of that shelter and out of the Revered. The dope and the booze were behind him too. They had to be or else Mr. Flannery wouldn't take him on. He had to pee in a cup just like everyone else, even though he was Flannery's nephew or third cousin or whatever. It was real big of Healy to make that introduction, to vouch for me like that. I wouldn't have done the same thing for him. I'm sure of it.

"Any luck?" the white cop asks me. He has that look, like no matter what I say it's going to be wrong.

"Nope," I tell him. "Not in there."

He looks at my lawyer.

The Hispanic cop takes his laptop back. "Thanks for trying," he says.

When they're gone I ask Slater what Sal Christaldi has said.

"He's still a bit groggy on the details," he tells me. "Maybe needs some time to recover from those injuries."

"What about the perjury charge?"

"The ADA's got other priorities right now," Slater says. "But that could change. All it takes is one detail to fall into place and the whole case gets reopened. My advice to you is the same advice I gave you before: if you know the kid's name, tell me. It's never too late."

When he's gone and I have the room to myself, a wave of relief washes over me. Maybe it's wrong to appreciate this stroke of luck, on account of it coming on the back of Sal Christaldi's injuries. Maybe those injuries have wiped out his memory. That would be sad. Tragic even. But it wasn't me who gave him those injuries. It was Pat Healy. I never touched the guy.

CHAPTER 13

Later in English class, while my teacher drones on, I start day-dreaming about my performance in that conference room. I wish Mr. Flannery could have seen me scan right past Healy's photo without flinching. Sure, I was flinching *inside*. I was pissing myself. But outside I was a tall cool glass of lemonade. Mr. Flannery was right. It's one thing to threaten someone with a perjury rap. It's another thing to make it stick. That ADA has nothing. She thought she could dangle six months and make me sing like a scared little punk, but she was wrong about that. Isaac West has nerves of steel.

It's stifling hot in that classroom. The low ceiling feels like a vice, and there are too many desks for the twelve kids, which makes it seem like a loser's birthday party. The teacher is this bald white buzzard named Mr. Perkins. He hates his job, and right now he's taking it out on this girl named Nyla, forcing her to stand up in front of everyone to read her "essay" on cats, which is just about the dumbest thing I've ever heard.

But even that can't wreck my mood. I'm golden. Ten days into my sentence, and all I have to do is keep my head down and keep my mouth shut, just like I promised Mr. Flannery. Haverland isn't so bad, now that I understand how it works. Most of the guys are pure scum, but as long as you stay out of their faces, they'll leave you alone. Maybe a punch or two here and there, just so some loser can make a point. But I can weather that. And I have no problem staying out of people's faces. It's one of my talents.

Twenty more days in here and I'll be back in the free and back on the plan. It's a good plan too. Maybe not the kind of plan any guidance counselor would recommend, but what do they know? They don't live in my world. In my world, the only power you have is the money you make. Most guys use it to buy themselves junk—cars, drugs, girls, gold teeth, dumbass chains to wear around their necks. Not Isaac West. I'm buying something better. Freedom. Not for myself either, but for Janelle. My own freedom will come later, after Janelle's squared away.

"Cats are clean because they always cleaning they-selves." Nyla's weave has come loose, leaving a strip of fuzz at her hair-line. She's still pretty though, tall and strong-looking. "And dogs eat they own mess so they're not clean at all." That's the gist of Nyla's essay. Cats are better than dogs.

My classes have been filled with Nylas all my life. She comes off about as smart as that stained whiteboard behind her. But you get that girl talking about something she cares about—her friends, her favorite rapper, some wild party she escaped right before the cops showed up—and she's as sharp as anyone. Mr. Perkins will never get at those smarts. He's not even trying. All he cares about is turning Nyla's four idiot sentences into a better essay, with a "thesis statement" and a "counterargument."

Personally, I agree with Nyla. Cats *are* better than dogs. They know how to keep to themselves. Dogs are always up in people's faces, begging for approval or picking fights with each other over territory, just like the losers in this place. I'll take a cat any old day.

The door opens and a guard pokes his head in. "Isaac West?"

Mr. Perkins scans the room. He has no idea which delinquent staring back at him is Isaac West. My first instinct is to hide under my desk. But I know that's pointless, so I raise my hand.

"Come with me," the guard says.

MS. JOMOLCA'S OFFICE IS so cramped there's barely enough room for me to pull out the green vinyl chair and sit. Her big metal desk is wedged in on a diagonal, and Ms. Jomolca, who barely reaches five feet, looks like she's been dropped in by a crane. I can hardly see her over the mountain of books, papers, and folders between us.

"You've had a busy couple of days," she says. "Meeting with your lawyer, a couple of detectives. Looked at some mug shots, did we?"

I nod. I'm not saying anything unless I have to.

"Did you bring your notebook? Are you carrying it everywhere?"

"Yup," I tell her. "It's right here."

She takes it from me and flips to the last page, where I've written my crime story.

"'I was bored one night so I decided to steal a car,'" she reads. "'It was late, blah blah blah.'" She scans down the page. "Okay, here we go. 'I punched him back once and he fell over and didn't get up. I got back in the car and drove it away.'" She turns to the next page, which is blank. "That's it?"

I nod.

"So where's the giant?"

"The what?"

"The *giant*. The white guy. The abominable snowman who was with you that night."

"Um, my lawyer said—"

"This has nothing to do with your lawyer. This is about you, Isaac, and the fact that this crime story is a fiction."

Ms. Jomolca has tiny adorable features, but when she's mad, she can scowl like nobody's business. There is nothing I can say that won't make an already shitty situation worse, so I keep my mouth shut.

"Was there or was there not another individual present?" she barks at me. She looks like she wants to launch herself over that desk and throttle me if I don't answer. All I can do is stare at my hands, like I always do, that damn giveaway. But I have to think before I answer. How much does she know? How much do I have to tell her? Will she go to the ADA? Is there a confidentiality thing here?

Finally she sighs. "Okay, let me ask you this, Isaac. Do you like it here?"

"Huh?" I look up.

"At Haverland. Do you like it here?"

"It's all right."

She's smirking now. "Really. Just all right? Not excellent? Not fantastic? Not so wonderful you want to stay here for as long as possible?"

A trick question. Obviously. But what's the right answer?

"It's . . . um . . . it's . . . fine?"

She digs through the pile of folders on her desk and pulls one out that has my name typed on the tab. She opens it and starts leafing through the papers. "Yeah, that's what I thought. Thirty days. You're here for thirty days, right?"

"Right."

"So am I to understand that thirty days isn't enough? You're hoping for more than that?"

My pulse picks up a little bit. "What are you saying?"

She shoves a stack of papers in my face. "What does that

say?" She fumbles around her desk for a highlighter, then marks up one word. "Read that."

"Contingent?"

"Contingent. Exactly. You do know what contingent means, right? Shall we look it up?" She types the word into her laptop. "Here we go. '*Contingent*: occurring or existing only if certain circumstances are the case; dependent on.'" She angles her laptop toward me so I can read it. "Do you understand what that means, Isaac?"

I nod. I can read. I'm not stupid.

"Your thirty-day sentence is *contingent* upon your successful completion of the program here," she says.

I nod again. "Okay."

She shakes her head. "No, it's not okay. Because you decided to come in here and lie. Don't even open your mouth right now. Just sit there and listen. I've been at this ten years, Isaac. Believe me, I can spot a liar. And thieves are the worst. Pimps, drug dealers? Nine times out of ten, they're so proud of what they've done, they can't wait to tell you all about it. But thieves, yeah, they know how to lie. And this?" She holds up my notebook. "I can't believe you thought you'd get something like this past us." She tears the offending page out of it. "Is this what you told the police?"

I blink at her.

"And they believed it?"

"Yes."

"Well that is some shoddy police work, but in here we have higher standards." She rips the page down the middle and tosses it into the trashcan. "As of now, we are in a bullshit-free zone. I don't care what you tell your lawyer or the police or the ADA. What I do care about is what you write in that notebook, and what you tell your team. Honesty is the only thing that matters in here, Isaac. You don't bring that to the table, then you don't get out of here in thirty days. Comprende?"

"Yes, Ms. Jomolca. I . . . wait, what?"

"This program is not voluntary. That's what I'm trying to tell you. It's a condition of your sentence. Why are you looking at me like that? Didn't your lawyer explain this to you?"

Slater never explained anything to me. He barely said a word that day in court. He spent all his time speaking to the judge in some language I couldn't understand. Thirty days was the takeaway. I understood that part just fine.

"See, how it works is I have to write up a report at the end of your sentence telling the judge how you did in here. And what the judge wants to hear is that you worked your program and came out a changed young man. And that's not some vague promise, Isaac. That's not you standing in front of the judge saying, 'Why, yes, Your Honor, I am a changed young man.' That's you working your program and being able to identify the errors you made. That's you taking full responsibility for those errors, understanding them, and equipping yourself with the mental and behavioral strategies to avoid them in the future."

Ms. Jomolca pauses, maybe to make sure I've understood so far. Yes, I understand. But I'm not sure what I'm supposed to say, if I'm supposed to say anything at all.

"The first order of business in all of that is telling the truth," she continues. "The *whole* truth. What have you got now, twenty days? That's not a lot of time. In fact, that may not be enough time to get through the layers of BS you have now introduced into this situation. You have basically wasted the first ten days of your program. No, worse than that, you've taken yourself backward. We've got to play catch up now just to get you back to where most kids start out.

So I'd suggest you get yourself busy, Mr. West." A brief smile flashes across her face. "Because I want to be able to write up a glowing report about you. I want to be able to use all my favorite words, like *transformation* and *renewed sense of empathy*. You know who else likes those words, Isaac?"

I shake my head. I want to understand her now.

"The judge. He hears words like that, they make him feel wise about handing down lenient sentences like the one you got. And believe me, Isaac, wise is how a judge wants to feel. You make him feel unwise, he'll send you back here until your eighteenth birthday."

"*What?*" I shout.

"Oh for crying out loud, Isaac, did your lawyer explain *anything* to you?"

My heart races. "He said thirty days."

"Yes. Thirty days, pending the successful completion of your program. You have to pay attention to the details. You have to ask questions when you don't understand something."

"But—"

"But nothing. Look, that's all behind you now anyway. That's the sentence you got, and if I were you, I wouldn't complain about it. You took the rap for sending a man into a coma, Isaac. If you ask me, that sentence was a gift. You're lucky you didn't wind up at Metro or John Jay. Haverland's a field day compared to where you could have been sentenced. Now, if you want to get out of here, you're going to have to give back. You do want to get out of here, right?"

My throat dries up. "Yes."

"Good. So here's what we're going to do. You have group in . . ." She checks the time on her phone. "Twelve minutes. That should be enough time. I'm going to sit here and you are going to rewrite your crime story while I watch."

She hands me the notebook along with a pen.

I stare at her openmouthed.

"Go ahead," she says. "Twelve minutes and counting. Either you write down what really happened that night, or you better make yourself comfortable in that cell of yours, because you're going to be there for a while."

CHAPTER 14

"Whenever you're ready, Isaac."

Dr. Horton does his best to sound reassuring, but it doesn't help. No matter how you look at it, I'm surrounded, ambushed. My so-called teammates are staring at me like I've personally insulted each and every one of them. Now it's payback time.

There's no point in stalling. The deed is done. The crime story is written, spilled out under Ms. Jomolca's nasty scowl. All that's left is to say it out loud.

May 27th. We drove to Waverly in my partner's pickup truck. We parked by the side of this vacant lot. Around the corner there was a cul de sac with four big mansions on it. We got out of the truck and just listened for half an hour. There were no lights on and nobody was making a sound. It was my job to handle the tow line, so I got that out of the back of the pick-up and hooked it up. Then we waited again to see if the noise woke anyone up. It was real quiet. All I could hear was the wind. We went to the driveway where the Escalade was parked. We knew the alarm was disabled, because it has this blinking red light inside that tells you when it's on.

My partner had set that up for us. Every night for two

weeks he went out there and threw pebbles at the Escalade to trigger the alarm. Mr. Christaldi was a heavy sleeper so it didn't always wake him up. But the neighbors got so pissed off about it they made him turn off the alarm. The way we got into the Escalade was I jammed a screwdriver between the glass and the window frame in the backseat. Then I held a blanket over the window and my partner punched it with his elbow. Then I climbed through and forced the shift into neutral. The driveway was on a slope so it started to roll. But I could steer it because there was no steering wheel lock. They left that off because they were so sure of their antitheft key code thing. They figured no one would ever get into the car in the first place. This wasn't a spur-of-the-moment-type job. We did our research. We knew what we were doing.

Once it was on the street, I had to jump out to help my partner push, then jump back in to steer. Back and forth like that till we got it all the way to that vacant lot.

My partner had done a lot of research on Mr. Christaldi too, so he knew what time he went to bed every night and that he was a heavy sleeper. But there was one thing he didn't know, which was that on that particular night, Mr. Christaldi's ex-wife had called to tell him she was marrying someone else. So even though all the lights in his house were off, Mr. Christaldi was actually awake drinking scotch in the dark while we broke into his Escalade. He watched us through his living room window the whole time.

So I was on my back hooking the Escalade up to the towline when I heard my partner say, "What the fuck?" in this really high voice.

Then I saw Mr. Christaldi wobbling toward us, barefoot, in his pajamas. He was wicked drunk. He went right up to my partner, who had about six inches on him, and tried to punch him. But he missed by a mile. The second time he tried to punch him, he tripped over his own feet and hit the pavement. He stayed down there for a while on his hands and knees, panting like a dog with his big stomach hanging out of his pajamas. I was watching from under the truck, waiting to see what he was going to do.

When he started to stand up, I could see my partner squaring up like he was gonna hit him this time. And I was like, no way man, don't get up. Just stay down there. But I didn't actually say that. I was basically hiding under that truck. Anyway, Mr. Christaldi was determined to get into something with my partner, I guess on account of being so drunk and not thinking straight.

So he gets to his feet again and he's swaying back and forth and squinting like he can barely see anything. Then he takes this sloppy swing at my partner, which misses completely. And that's when my partner punches him, right on the side of the head. Mr. Christaldi jumps backwards like he's about to fall and I keep waiting for him to hit the dirt, but his feet just keep moving real fast, like he's running backwards.

And I'm thinking, okay, that's it. Let's just go. Forget the stupid Escalade. The job is fucked. Then my partner starts looking around on the ground, and I'm thinking he's looking for his keys, so I start to slide out from under the Escalade, thinking, good, let's just blow this.

But then I see Mr. Christaldi wobbling back to us, so I slide back under the truck.

Now this time Mr. Christaldi takes his time setting up for a punch. He stands there like a boxer with his fists in front of him, concentrating real hard like he's waiting for the right moment. And that's when I see the rock in my partner's hand. That's what he was looking for on the ground. Not his keys.

I don't know what he was thinking. I mean we chose that car because it was supposed to be easy. It was a no-contact-type boost. And it was set up perfectly. With the alarm disabled and everything. But still, I'm thinking—hoping, actually praying—that my partner's just gonna use that rock to scare Mr. Christaldi, maybe just show it to him, get him to back off and go home. But he's got other ideas.

So while I'm lying under that truck, he reels back and bashes Mr. Christaldi on the side of the head.

Mr. Christaldi spins all the way around on one foot, like a ballerina or something. Then he hits the dirt real hard and his head comes down right where my partner nailed him with that rock.

My partner drops the rock in the back of the pickup truck, which is the loudest thing I've ever heard. Then he tells me to hurry up and hook up the tow. Mr. Christaldi is lying right next to me. His eyes are closed and blood is oozing out of his head. Then my partner finds another rock and slides it under his head like a pillow.

And I'm thinking how's that supposed to help? My partner has his sleeves pulled down over his hands like he's trying to keep his fingerprints off of it. At the time I was too freaked out to make sense of it, but I guess he was covering his tracks, trying to make it look like he landed on that rock.

So I get the chain hooked up and everything else goes just like we planned, me steering the Escalade, my partner driving the pickup. As we're driving away, I keep looking in the rearview mirror, trying to figure out if Mr. Christaldi is breathing. But all I can see is his big stomach hanging out of his pajamas like a beach ball with half the air missing. And I can't tell if it's moving up and down or not because it's too dark. Then we turn a corner and I can't see him anymore.

I close the notebook and sit back in my chair. Nobody says anything for a minute. They're all sizing me up, seeing if I flinch.

"So who's this *partner*?" Barbie says eventually. "He got a name? He a friend of yours?"

I turn to Dr. Horton. I had no time to strategize about my crime story this time around. With Ms. Jomolca scowling at me, I had to move that pen or else she'd know I was tap dancing around the truth. But then a funny thing happened. As soon as I brought that pen down on the paper, I realized I could tell the truth about that night. The truth was already out there thanks to Mr. Christaldi. Sure there was another guy, a white kid, a "giant." That didn't mean I had to write down his name. It was the perfect workaround. Nothing I wrote was a lie, and none of it put Healy in any danger.

"Isaac," Dr. Horton says. "Would you like to answer Barbie's question?"

"Do I have to?"

"So you still hiding things," Barbie says. "You still holding out on us."

"He's protecting his partner's identity," Wayne says. "Ain't that right? What did you do, take the rap for him or something?"

I face Dr. Horton again.

"You don't have to reveal any names if you don't want to," Dr. Horton says. "That's up to you. But you do have to answer your teammates' questions. Even if the answer is, 'I don't want to answer that.'"

"Okay," I say. "Yeah, I took the rap for him."

"Why?" Riley asks.

"He was eighteen. I was fifteen when it happened."

"So you did him a solid," Wayne says.

"But why?" Barbie asks. "That's what I want to know. Big

risk you taking the rap for putting a guy in a coma. He *is* in a coma, right? Or did you lie about that too?"

She's so sure I'm holding out on her, like the story I just told isn't enough. There has to be something even worse. I have to give the girl credit. Barbie Santiago knows a thing or two about the world. Whatever reason she had for icing that ponketo, Enrique Cabron, I'm sure it came on the heels of a long and storied youth in crime. Her instincts are sharp in the way only the street can sharpen them. But that doesn't mean they can cut through Isaac West. There are things about me she'll never know.

"Nah," I tell her. "That's all true. He's in a coma and it was my partner who put him there. Not me."

Barbie locks those amber eyes onto mine in a death grip I couldn't have broken even if I wanted to. The temperature in the room goes way up, but only in that shaft of air between her and me. Then her mouth curls up in that half smile of hers, a smile that says "come here" and "fuck off" at the same time. And there's that gold tooth again. Man, how I hate that gold tooth.

"All right," she says. "Now we on to something."

CHAPTER 15

The next day in computer class, I get an email from Janelle. She's been using the computers at school and the library for years. She's already a pro. Her school reports are expertly researched, perfectly spelled, and full of the same little charts and graphs Deon likes so much. She's a master of extra credit. I'm still a newbie and I get stupid excited when I see her name in my inbox, like I must be breaking a rule reaching across time and space into the free like that just to talk to her.

But then Stanley Huang comes over.

"Work first," he says. "Rule number one, remember?" He sits in the chair next to me, angles the laptop his way, and closes out my email window. Together, we slog through another session of word processing. They're just words. What do they need to be "processed" for? About half an hour into it, Huang gets bored, lobs a few lame insults at me, then leaves me with a tutorial to do on my own, if I can "handle it."

I handle it by opening Janelle's email the second Stanley Huang turns his back.

I'm so glad you're finally on email. Now we can talk like every day. Yay! Okay don't get mad. And don't worry because I'm really okay, I promise promise, but I have to tell you that I'm not living with Mom anymore. I kind of ran away. Mom's gone down the sinkhole again and I'm sorry to say that I am simply not going to stick around and take her crap anymore. She's drunk all the time. Half the time she's passed out. Doesn't matter who's knocking on the door. They're coming all hours now looking for her. You know how they get. So I dumped her gin down the sink and oh my God when she figured that one out she tried to hit me. Don't worry though because she was so drunk she could barely see straight. She kept going on and on about the hammers in her head. You know how she does that. Then she broke the lock on my door. You know that padlock you got me? I came home from school and it was gone. The door won't even close now. It just swings open. And you know I'm not staying there if I can't even close the door. Right now I'm staying with Daniela. Her Mom said it was okay for a little while but she doesn't want to get in trouble. She's super strict but I think she likes me because I help with the baby, who's two and a half and sooooo cute. I guess in a way it's like my first baby-sitting job only instead of getting paid I'm getting food and a place to sleep. We have Cuban food every night and you would not believe it but rice can actually taste really good. I share a room with Daniela and her ten-year-old sister who's always playing with my hair. The only thing I'm worried about is that Mom will call the police or show up at school and make me go home with her. I don't want to start skip-ping school, but I'm not sure what to do. I can't live with her anymore, Isaac. You know I can't. You know I had to do this.

"Um, Isaac? Did you finish that tutorial?"
It's Huang, hanging over me like a shadow.
"What? Yeah," I lie.

"The whole thing? It's like half an hour long. At least. Probably more like an hour." Huang stabs his skinny arms across my air space and taps at the keyboard. "You paused it. You're not supposed to check email until you've done your work." He makes sure this is loud enough for Mr. Klein to hear. Klein hears, but for some reason he doesn't feel like making a big deal out of it. So I shoulder Huang's hand away and type out a reply to my sister.

hang on Janelle i'll figure something out, don't worry stay with mrs rodriguez.

Then, with both Huang and Mr. Klein eyeballing me, I settle in for another half hour of word processing.

CHAPTER 16

Out in the yard that day, I sit against the wall with my note-book open over my knees. I'm not writing anything, but if anyone's looking (and hopefully no one is), I'll look busy, rather than just alone. A kid sitting alone is an easy target. I'm thinking about Janelle. It's better for her to be living with Mrs. Rodriguez than my mom. The lady sounds solid. If she'll just let Janelle stay there for another nine days, that'll be perfect. I'll be home after that, so I can run interference between Janelle and my mother.

When my mother goes down the sinkhole, she has a real mean streak, especially for Janelle. She *hates* Janelle. It doesn't make any sense. Janelle is much nicer to her than I am. Plus she never gets in trouble at school. Maybe it's jeal-ousy, on account of Janelle being so pretty or so smart. Maybe my mother just blames Janelle for our father leaving. It was that second pregnancy that did him in, made him rethink the whole "family thing." My mom loves telling that story.

There's a sudden outburst of swearing on the other side of the yard.

Two half-court basketball games are on. The games are rough and dirty. There's no referee. They referee them-selves. And they don't care about a stray elbow or two. Over by the foul line, I spot Cardo standing alone with his hands stuffed into the waistband of his red scrubs. The rest of the Disciples are watching the other game. I stuff my notebook in my waistband and make my way over.

"Hey man," I say. "I thought you were out of here. Didn't you have your court date?"

Cardo nods but he keeps his eyes on that game, like maybe he has money riding on it.

"So what happened? Where've you been?"

"Solitary." He tears his eyes from the game just long enough for something to flash behind them—rage maybe. Then it dies back down, like there's no point to it. "It's where they send you when you get bad news. So you don't kill yourself."

Bad news? That could mean anything. A death in the family, something about his pregnant girlfriend. I wait for him to fill me in, but Cardo just keeps watching that basketball game. It's a mean one. The players charge through each other and hit the pavement like it's nothing. "You're still getting out of here, though, right?"

"Yeah, I'm getting out of here. In about six months."

"Six months? Man, that sucks. Your girlfriend's uncle gonna hold that job for you?"

Cardo shakes his head. "In six months, I'm being tried as an adult. Facing thirty to life. At Walpers. It's just like my man, Mig, says. Early release is for snowflakes and pussies. Disciples they like to keep around."

"But—"

"Don't hassle *me*, brother. You don't like how it sounds, take it up with the judge."

Over by the other game, the Disciples spot me with one of their own. Mig, the older one with the crescent-shaped scar, motions for them to follow, and they all start making their way over, slowly, spread out in loose clusters to take up as much space as possible. When Cardo sees them coming, he straightens up to his full height, about an inch taller than me. The Disciples form a ragged half circle at his back. Flavio Pendon, the guy who went after me in the cafeteria, looks like he's ready for his rematch.

"You on your own now," Cardo tells me. "I can't be holding your hand in here, no'm saying? If you smart, you get your own people, stop moping around all solo and shit."

Chuckles from the Disciples behind him, then some Spanish I can't understand.

"What's up with that anyway?" Cardo says. "Even that child fucker O'Neil got peeps. Why don't you hang with him?"

More chuckles. Cardo's warming up.

"Why you don't play hoops at least?" He motions to the game behind me. "You *half* black, right?"

The Disciples crack up at this one, like no one's ever made a basketball joke about a black kid before. I suck at hoops. It's not my thing. Ask me how fast I can jump in and out of an Escalade with a broken window though. Ask me how fast I can boost a carton of cigarettes from a 7-Eleven. But there's no point getting into it with Cardo. He's fronting. Being real obvious about it too. I can't hold it against him. He's just trying to get back with the Disciples. Now that he's stuck here, they're all he has. And he's got some making up to do. All that stuff about starting over in Miami? That was bullshit just like they said. And they're eating it up now. Because they're so smart. Because they know *everything*.

"Yeah, maybe I'll give hoops a try," I tell him. "Good luck with the Disciples, man. I hope it's a real successful collaboration."

This is not the response Cardo was hoping for. Something in the air goes still, prickly, like it's getting ready for something big. A few of the Disciples look at each other. Flavio Pendon looks like he's ready to jump straight out of his skin and stab me to death with his raw bones. It's only Mig's putting a hand in front of him that keeps that dog on the leash. I know I've got to walk a fine line here.

"No, I mean it," I say. "I'm sorry things didn't work out for you in court. I know how it is. But I hope you get everything you want, man. I really do."

Cardo's still glaring at me when I turn my back on him.

He's pissed off because he failed to make me slink away like a little punk. But you know what, Cardo? Isaac West is no punk. And I'm not the rookie you think I am. This is not the first time some fool tried to score points on me to impress his posse. Sean McKenzie tried the same thing. Now his nose is a different shape.

Not that I like fighting. I hate it. Most times it's bullshit and easy to avoid. But if I've learned anything in this zoo, it's that you can *never* let folks think you're easily punked, because they will take you up on that shit. Again and again and again. So I walk the line. I walk the line like the pro this hellhole is making me. By the time I'm finished at Haverland, *I'll* be the expert in surviving juvie, and everyone can come to me for advice. Only I won't be around to give it, because I'll be back in the free.

I head back to that patch of wall and open my notebook again. My heart is thumping like a freight train, but I don't look up to see if anyone has noticed. That's a rookie move. The trick is to sit down like you own the place and get busy with something. It doesn't matter what. In sixth grade I used to carry around a broken Blackberry I found in the trash just so I'd have something to tap at while I walked through the halls. That way I didn't have to look at anyone; eventually, they stopped looking at me. Nobody can make himself more invisible than Isaac West. How do you think I manage to steal so much stuff?

I'm like a ghost, a mirage. Some kid you half remember drifting through your apartment building or your school. But you forget his name and you don't spend too much time trying to remember it because you know you'll never see him again anyway.

CHAPTER 17

"So all I have to do is lie there?"

Dr. Horton has set up two chairs to act as the pickup and the Escalade. I'm going to play myself lying between them, hooking up the tow line, while Wayne plays Healy.

"We need a name," Wayne says. "I'm gonna play this guy I can't just be *partner*."

"How about Connor?" Riley offers.

"The hell kind of name is that?" Wayne asks. "Do I look like a Connor? This kid a brother, right? You know any brothers named Connor?"

"Actually," Riley says. "Isaac never told us his race, so why are you assuming he's black?"

"Yeah, Wayne," Barbie jumps in. "Maybe this partner of his some white dude. Don't be such a racist."

"Actually," Riley says. "Who said his partner was male?"

"Yeah, Wayne," Barbie says, smiling so that her gold tooth flashes. "Now you're being racist *and* sexist. What's up with that?"

"Why don't we just let Wayne pick a name," Dr. Horton says. "Unless you have a preference, Isaac?"

I do not have a preference, and the fact that they're all assuming my partner is black is an added bonus.

"Fine," Wayne says. "Then call me Andre."

Barbie stifles a laugh so noisily it makes everyone else laugh.

"The hell's wrong with Andre?" Wayne asks.

"Nothing," Barbie says, still laughing.

"Okay, so who's playing Mr. Christaldi?" Dr. Horton asks, sounding tired.

Javier raises his hand. "I'll do it. I don't mind getting beat."

"Yeah, you a little *too* into that, you ask me," Barbie says.

"I didn't ask you," Javier replies coolly.

Wayne digs through the cardboard box and comes out with a yellow Nerf football. He puts it on the floor next to Sandra's chair. "I got my rock. Let's do it."

WE BEGIN THE ROLE-PLAY right before Healy punches Mr. Christaldi. According to Dr. Horton, that and everything that comes after is the "meat of the matter."

The theft itself and all the planning that went into it is something we'll get to, "time permitting." This is great news for me. The last thing I want to do is invite these vultures into Mr. Flannery's operation. That would mean a whole new round of lying, and I'm crystal clear on how that turns out.

Javier is pretty good at acting drunk, but he doesn't look anywhere near as pathetic as Mr. Christaldi did that night. Christaldi was like one of those slow-moving flies you could swat with your bare hands. Javier just looks like he's stumbling home after a killer party.

Wayne, though, has Healy down cold. He's got the same fire in his eyes, like he's in control most of the time but one wrong move and watch out. That was the thing with Healy. He was great at planning. "Slow and methodical," according to Mr. Flannery. Healy had a whole notebook full of information on Mr. Christaldi, so much he said he knew him better than his own friends. And he went over the plan with me about twenty times that night before we even rolled up to that cul-de-sac. Great at planning, but the second something went wrong, he lost it. You can't be like that if you're going to steal things for a living. Shit goes wrong and you've got to roll with it.

"What the fuck?" Wayne calls out.

Javier swings at him and misses. When he settles down and gets his footing again, Wayne tap-punches him on the side of the head. "Bam!" he says.

Javier jumps and runs backward all the way to the wall— just like I wrote in my notebook. When he comes back toward Wayne with his fists up like a boxer's, Wayne picks up that Nerf football and taps him on the ear. "Bam!"

This time Javier hits the floor. Hard.

"Okay right there," Dr. Horton says. "Isaac, what are you thinking?"

"Um, I'm thinking this is nuts. We shouldn't even be here."

"But you don't do nothin'?" Barbie says. "You didn't try to stop it?"

"It all happened so fast."

"Did it?" Dr. Horton asks. "Okay, let's try it again. Wayne, Javier, I want you to slow it down. Isaac, I want you to put yourself in each individual moment and tell us what you felt. Not what you were thinking. What you *felt*."

This time through, Wayne stops after that first punch, the one without the rock.

"Isaac?" Dr. Horton says.

"Surprised?" I tell him.

"Good." Dr. Horton motions for Wayne and Javier to continue.

Javier wobbles over with his fists up. Wayne rears back real big, then taps him on the ear with that Nerf football.

"Isaac?" Dr. Horton presses.

"Afraid, I guess."

"What else? Close your eyes and take yourself back there."
I do as I'm told. "Frustrated," I tell him. "Like . . . like . . ."

"Go on," Dr. Horton says. "Dig into it. Frustrated like
what?"

I try to put myself back there, lying on the asphalt
underneath that car, with all those little rocks digging
into my back, the vacant lot spreading out beside me like
a dark puddle, the tow chain lying heavy across my legs.

This is called "visualization." It's supposed to help you
reconnect with the moment. They have all kinds of tricks to
send you back to the worst moments of your life. You're supposed to use all your senses. Remember how cold or hot you
were. Remember what you heard, what you smelled. Smell is
a big one. I can remember what it smelled like underneath
that Escalade. Grease and gasoline. But I wish I couldn't. If I
had my way, the night of May 27 would disappear forever—
not just from my own memory, but from everybody's.

"Isaac?" Dr. Horton says.

"I'm thinking." I know I have to perform for these people,
give them something they can paw and pick through. Otherwise Ms. Jomolca won't write up a good report on me. I
remember the chill in the air that night, the sound of the
wind in some trees, a helpless feeling, like an ache in my
chest. Was it helplessness? Maybe not. I could have slid out
from under that Escalade. I wasn't trapped there. It wasn't
part of the plan to hide like that. But Mr. Christaldi hadn't
seen me yet. At least not my face.

"I'm thinking I'm safe down there. I'm thinking don't
jump into this. It's not yours."

"Hit him again," Dr. Horton says.

Wayne tosses the Nerf ball a few times then reaches way
back to set up for the punch.

"Stop," Dr. Horton says. "That second. Right there. Could you see that he was going to hit Mr. Christaldi with that rock?"

"Yeah."

"And how did you feel?"

"I guess I was thinking that—"

"No, not what you were thinking. What you were *feeling*."

I squeeze my eyes shut. There were so many thoughts running through my head that night. But what was I *feeling*? I wasn't sure I felt anything. I didn't want to watch Mr. Christaldi die. I remember that much. I didn't want to live with that. "Sad?" I say. "Maybe I was feeling sad?"

"Maybe?" Dr. Horton asks.

"No. Definitely. I was definitely feeling sad."

"Why? What were you sad about?"

"I guess because I knew what was about to happen to Mr. Christaldi and I couldn't stop it."

Barbie snorts. "Couldn't?"

There isn't an ounce of pity in those amber eyes. Just the heavy weight of everything she knows. But in that moment I know it too. It wasn't sadness I felt that night. It was shame. Because I could have stopped it. If I'd have told Healy to put down that rock, he probably would have. Healy was panicking. The plan was blown up and he didn't know what to do. I should have stepped up. It didn't matter that I was the "junior partner." I should have risen to the occasion. Instead I hid under that Escalade like a scared little punk and let Healy drive the whole job right over a cliff.

"Right there." Dr. Horton is pointing at me now. "That's it."

"What?"

"Whatever you're feeling. That's what we work with. Let's go again, from the beginning."

We replay the scene maybe a dozen times after that, slowing it down, "digging into it," trying to bring me back to that moment where I should have done something but didn't.

It's not about solving anything or finding the answer to why it all happened. It's about breaking that moment down into the smallest possible parts. It's not enough to say I was sad or scared or frustrated, or even guilty and full of shame. Those are just words. They're "closed doors." They want those doors opened. They want to know what all of those things feel like. In my muscles, in my head. In my chest and my stomach. They want to peel me open and shine a light into parts of myself I don't want to face, parts I've buried deep. They want to make me see it all. When they're through with me (and that blessed day cannot come soon enough), they'll have me seeing things that will make me tremble with fear. That's their promise. And I'm beginning to believe them.

CHAPTER 18

On Saturday a guard tells me I have another visitor. I never realized how popular being in juvie would make me. I figured I'd be spending these thirty days alone, keeping my head down, enjoying the delicious food. I'm hoping it's Janelle. But when the buzzer goes, the person who stumbles toward me kills any hope I had.

My mother is hunched over, pale as a ghost, and even skinnier than the last time I saw her. The red roots of her frizzled blond hair are two inches long, and that's not a fashion statement. That's her spending her bleach money on booze. She has to stop halfway for a coughing fit that shakes the building. When she goes down the sinkhole, she does it in style. After she's coughed up half a lung, she slides into the bench across from me and takes out her pack of Virginia Slims.

A guard who must have seen this move a million times shakes his head at her.

She glares at him, but she puts them back in the pocket of her dirty fleece jacket. Yellow with Playboy bunny ears sewn on the chest because, yeah, she's definitely hot enough to work for that organization.

"It's freezing in here," she says.

She's lost another tooth. That makes four. She looks like poor white trash in the best of circumstances. Now she's starting to look like a hillbilly. I wonder if she pulled it her-self, or if she found some way to get past her fear of the free clinic ("all the wrong people there") and had it profession-ally yanked.

"So where is she?"

That's her greeting. Not *Hello.* Not *How are you?* Not *Are they treating you okay?* or *Have you been beaten and/or raped while incarcerated?*

"I don't know where she is."

"But you're not surprised I'm asking, which means you know she ran away. So how's that work? She tell you she ran away, but she didn't tell you where she's staying?" My mother presses her lips together, which brings out the smoker's wrin-kles above them. She is the oldest-looking thirty-two-year-old in the world. She looks more like sixty-two.

The stupid thing is, it wouldn't be that hard for her to find Janelle. She's at school all day, for shit's sake. Her name's on a register. Then again, it's not out of the question that my mother doesn't know which middle school Janelle goes to, or what grade she's in, for that matter. For once, her shittiness as a parent is working for us.

My mother coughs again. "I don't believe you, Isaac. That girl tells you everything."

"She didn't tell me where she was. What does it matter anyway as long as she's safe?"

"Is she living in *a car*? Is she sleeping *on the street*?"

"All I know is that she's safe. Is that why you came here?"

She tries to run her yellow fingers through her hair, but they get stuck in a knot. She's drunk, but only a little. The smell of booze is strong but it can't mask the cigarettes, and even those two stinks working together can't drown out the stench of that vanilla perfume she always wears. What does she think she is, dessert?

"Well, I came here to see how my *son* was doing, if that's okay with you."

My mother will sometimes say the words *son* and *daughter* really loud like the only problem in our relationship is that we've forgotten how we're related to her.

"I'm fine," I tell her. "And so's Janelle."

"Oh really. Did you know she's been sneaking out of the apartment ever since you left? She thought I didn't notice those plastic crates, but I did. Now what kind of girl goes out at night like that and doesn't come home?"

The correct answer is: the kind of girl who wants to be as far away from *you* as possible. But I don't say that. I have to think strategically. If I play it right, this little visit could work out perfectly.

"I know, right?" I say. "She can be so willful."

The word *willful* is straight out of my mother's playbook, right next to *spoilt*, *cushy*, and *charmed*. The woman sincerely believes Janelle and I are living it up in some Disneyland of comfort and security, thanks to her ace parenting. That's how divorced from reality she is. The two haven't seen each other in years. My strategy seems to work though. She softens a bit, which leaves room for the one part of her wrecked face that still has some life in it—a twinkle of mischief in her eye.

"Sometimes, I swear to God, I just want to knock some *sense* into that girl."

"Me too," I lie.

"She's a good student and all, but she *lacks common sense.*"

"Yup."

"It don't matter what your grades are if you're running all over town. You got to be *street* smart."

"Which she definitely is not."

Janelle is actually the best kind of street smart, the kind

that stays *off* the streets. Janelle's happiest with her nose in a book or her butt in a sports uniform. If there's a half hour free between volleyball and choir practice, she'll spend it in the school library, getting a jump start on the next day's math lesson. Where she gets this I have no idea. It sure as hell skipped me.

"She got a lot of her father in her, you know," my mother says. "Always dreaming."

I nod along, like, yeah, I've always thought that about my father. Like I know *anything* about the guy. My mother won't tell me shit, except how he ran out on us. She can get real specific about that. How she went looking for him at the donut shop where he worked, and his boss was all pissed about him not showing up for the commuter rush. How she couldn't track him down because he never introduced her to his family. How they never had a real wedding because it was too expensive. To me, that all adds up to a guy who was never planning to stay. But it doesn't tell me anything about who he is. She even burned all his pictures.

Sometimes I look in the mirror and try to subtract my mother just to figure out what he looks like. But it never works. All I ever see is her there, plus some extra pigment from my father. Other than that, he's a black hole.

"She's not like us," my mother says. "You and me, I mean. She expects too much. She doesn't understand how the world works."

"I know. She takes everything for granted."

Another one from my mother's hit list. Ordinary things like a roof over your head, sheets, and a toilet are not things a thirteen-year-old girl is supposed to expect. They're luxuries, privileges. The undeserved gifts of a hardworking mother. Whatever. I let her have it. We need to be in league now, working together against Janelle with her "spoilt," "unrea-sonable" demands.

"So maybe this is a blessing in disguise?" I suggest.

But she's not buying it. Not yet.

"I'm just saying, maybe she should get a taste of what it's like without you to take care of her."

"Hah!"

"See what it's like in the real world."

"She'd never survive."

"And I bet you could use a break, right? Focus on yourself for once? Maybe do rehab again?"

"Oh don't start with that."

"No, I'm just saying—"

"I do not need *rehab*."

"I know. I was just thinking maybe—"

"You know what, Isaac? The last thing I need right now is a lecture from you. I've got enough going on."

"I'm not lecturing you."

"You're always lecturing me. Yes, you are and don't deny it. You think you know what's what. Well let me tell you some-thing—"

"Mom, I'm just saying—"

"Shut up, Isaac. You don't know shit!"

The same guard looks over with a warning.

My mother absorbs his glare with a sniff, then lowers her voice. "Just stop bullshitting me, okay? I'm in no mood. Where is she?"

And just like that I've lost her. I should have spent more time in her corner, more time criticizing Janelle. My moth-er's favorite hobby is criticizing Janelle. How could I have forgotten that? I should have ragged on Janelle's "stuck-up attitude," her "selfish" demands, how "privileged" she is with her after-school activities—all the demented complaints my mother has about Janelle. They're so insane it wouldn't have cost me a dime to spit them back at her. But I rushed things and now I've lost her.

"Mom, I want Janelle to be safe too."

She snorts.

"Oh come on. When have I ever wanted anything else?"

"You don't know what's best for that girl. You're not her mother."

"All I'm saying is maybe the two of you could use a break from each other."

As she sizes me up, I can't help myself. I dare to hope that some part of her will jump at the chance to let both of us go—maybe to focus on rehab or, more likely, to drown herself in gin. No matter how crap you are as a mother, it still must be hard raising two kids on your own. Hell, I'm offering her a vacation, something she probably thinks she deserves.

But her face turns from suspicious to bitter. She doesn't want a vacation; she wants company. That's what Janelle is to her now that I'm in juvie: a companion, a sounding board. If she had a boyfriend to complain to or a friend to confide in, she wouldn't be here searching for Janelle at all. She might not even have noticed Janelle was missing or that I'm locked up. But living alone in that pigsty of an apartment, with no one to clean up after her and no one to complain to about the mess? No way am I selling that to her. I should have known. Now I've made her my enemy. She's pissed at me for trying to manipulate her, just like she's pissed at the world for its never-ending shitstorm of bad luck.

No one has ever been unluckier than Karen West. Just ask her. Good luck rang her bell once, realized it was *her* living there, and split before she opened the door.

Boo-effing-hoo.

My mother has never, not once in all my life, taken a single scrap of responsibility for the shit that happens to her. No matter how many times I've dragged her passed-out ass off the bathroom floor or mopped up her puke, she's always the victim. She can wake up from a stone-cold blackout midtirade and not once spare a thought for her own contribution to the situation. She even blamed the gin once for being "so goddamn full of alcohol."

"I'm telling you the girl is trouble," she tells me. "I know you like to pretend she's a little angel, but come on." She forces a little *putt-putt* of a laugh through those thin lips. "You know as well as I do that she ain't no angel." Her cold blue eyes pin me to that bench. "Isn't that right, Isaac."

A flash of something goes through me. Ice water. Or fire. A voice in my head hisses a single word:

Ashland.

That's how it comes to me when it comes, like a snake winding itself around my ankles.

Ashland.

It never goes away for good. It always comes back.

Ashland.

Sometimes it settles like a cold draft and I can't shake it off, can't get warm.

If I was in the orange-rug room right now, Dr. Horton would be pointing that finger at me and saying, "That! Right there. Let's focus on that."

But I can't. Ashland is a place I can never return to.

Even though I'm always there.

I slump onto the table, catch my forehead on my fists.

"Aww, come on, Isaac," my mother says.

"Why can't you just leave her alone?" It comes out like a whimper.

"Don't be stupid. I need her. You know that. Things ain't

right at home. I'm sick. My insides are damaged. I can't do it no more."

"Then stop."

"And how we supposed to eat?"

I lift my head off the table and look at her, try to find a wavelength we can share, some way to get her to understand me, to understand the way the rest of the world thinks. "Why don't you just get a job?"

This shuts her right down. "Why don't you mind your business? Get a job. Yeah, like they're just dropping out of the trees. What the hell do you know? Get a job. Nobody's offering jobs to me, Isaac. We are broke. In case you didn't notice. And you know they're going to throw us out of that apartment. It's not free. It's only subsidized. And them damn neighbors . . ."

She goes on for a while about the stoners next door— how nosy they are and what hypocrites. Smoking pot all day, then complaining about the so-called noise she makes. I let her speak because there's nothing I can do now. I'm at the bottom of my own sinkhole, staring up at her like I'm about to be flushed. That's what it's like to be Karen West's son. It's like drowning in slow motion.

But that's nothing. It's even worse to be her daughter.

She rambles on and on. She can go for hours. Ticking off all the ways the world is screwing her. It's the same list, with different names. Landlords, neighbors, people looking at her funny, people judging. I try to block out her voice so I won't remember any of the names. I don't want those people in my head. And I can't take her side anymore. I can't even pretend to. It costs too much. I've got nothing left.

"Janelle's got to come back to me. I really need her right now." My mother slouches forward, trying to draw me back. She likes it when I take her side. It's what she craves more than anything: a united front against all enemies, especially Janelle.

God, how she hates Janelle.

But her voice is noise now, a mindless hum of empty sounds, pure nonsense. I know why she needs Janelle back. She doesn't have to say it. She *can't* say it. She doesn't have that kind of courage. But she knows I know. She makes *me* think it. Makes me dig it up out of that box where I keep it. The one labeled *Ashland*. The one buried deep at the bottom of my soul, beneath the rot and a thick layer of forgetting that only sometimes works.

CHAPTER 19

It's cold and bright out in the yard the next day. I roam the perimeter on my own for a while, let Cardo and the Disciples give me the stink eye. There's nothing to be gained from challenging me. I'm small-time. As soon as I'm back in the free, they'll forget all about me. And I'll be there soon, fourteen days to be exact, which is a hell of a lot better than what Cardo's facing. I sit down with my notebook and pretend to write.

A few seconds later there's a commotion by the entrance to the yard. A few catcalls and some whistles, then Stanley Huang shuffles out into the harsh sunlight like a quivering noodle. The rest of the geeks follow him, trying to be invisible. And failing. Badly. The geeks almost never come out to the yard. They have some arrangement with the warden that lets them stay in the computer room. But here they all are, venturing out into "the rectangle of pain," as they like to call it. They look as out of place as they must feel, like china teacups set loose in a cage of hammers.

When Deon spots me, he whacks Huang on the chest then leads everyone over.

I close my eyes and brace myself. The geeks are of no use to me out in the yard. Even sitting with them at lunch is only slightly better than sitting alone. When they arrive,

Little Anthony, a skinny white Italian kid from Revere who's no bigger than Janelle's stuffed Tigger, hugs his arms against the cold and bounces on his toes. "Man, it's cold out here." *Here* comes out as *heeyah*.

Deon tells him to stop being such a pussy.

Salim, a Pakistani stringbean, stops shivering too. He's scared of Deon. He's scared of everything, and I don't blame him. He's got wide black eyes and probably weighs even less than Anthony. I wonder if he'll survive in here. I wonder what put him here in the first place.

"What the hell are you guys doing?" I ask them in a low voice.

"We got something to tell you," Deon says.

I look at Huang. "What? Are you kicking me out of the computer class or something?"

"Nobody's kicking anybody out," Deon says. "But listen, Little Anthony's been reading your emails, and—"

"What?"

"Chill out," Deon says. "Little Ant reads everyone's emails."

Little Anthony, still shivering but with his arms pressed to his sides, nods. "I have problems with boundaries."

"Yeah," Deon says. "You need to get over the whole privacy thing."

"Privacy's so last century," Huang adds.

So the prick's a philosopher too. Good for him.

"Anyway," Deon says. "Little Ant showed me and Huang and we decided to do some research."

Huang gestures toward the redhead. "It was mostly Fitzpatrick."

Fitzpatrick is busy scanning the yard for anything that looks like a threat, which is basically everything and everyone. "Yeah," he says. "We were wondering if you've thought about foster care for your sister, 'coz, like maybe your mother's not in a position to take care of her right now?"

I'm still pretty freaked out about the fact that they've been reading my emails. The idea that this band of criminal nerds is in possession of intimate personal details about my family is something I can't even make room for yet. I'm going to have to take some time over that one.

"What? Because she's a drunk?" I say.

"Well, yeah," Fitzpatrick says. "That and the fact that she's . . ."

Fitzpatrick is a wise man not to finish that sentence.

"Anyway," he goes on. "That Mrs. Rodriguez lady, she could apply to be Janelle's foster mother. Make the whole thing legit."

"Get some money out of it too," Deon adds.

"See, my brother's in foster care," Fitzpatrick explains. "And his foster mom, Julia, she's this really nice lady over in Saugus, and she said she'd help walk Mrs. Rodriguez through the whole process. She says a lot of the Hispanics do this kind of thing for free, but if they went through the right channels, they could get money from the state. You just have to prove your mother's unfit."

I laugh. If there's a guidebook on how to be an unfit mother, Karen West's picture is on the cover. Unfit mothers the world over could learn a thing or two from Karen West.

"That guidance counselor your sister mentioned should be able to help with that too," Little Anthony says. "The one at her school? He seems to be taking a real interest in her. That'll help."

"So you've read *all* of my emails?"

"Except for the spam. You need to upgrade your fil—"

Little Anthony was going to say "filter." I know this because I've heard people batting the word around in the computer room. But Little Anthony never has the chance to finish the word or the thought, because he's too busy getting thrown away—and by that I mean being literally lifted off the ground and tossed aside like crumpled-up garbage—by Flavio Pendon. Little Anthony isn't even his target. He's just in the way. Pendon is coming for me, all the while machine-gunning something in Spanish I can't understand.

There's no way out of this one. It's either fight this psycho or let everyone see me run away like a pussy. So I get ready, ball my hands into fists. I figure I'll go straight for the throat, one punch. Maybe that'll be enough to get him on the ground. Maybe the guards will see it before the rest of the Disciples jump in. That's my only hope, because if the Disciples decide they want me on the ground, or under it, I'm history. And nothing my new geek friends have to say on the subject will make any difference.

It's my lucky day, though. Miracle of miracles: I'm not Pendon's target either.

Salim is. Salim actually has a couple of inches on Pendon, but they're a scrawny couple of inches, nothing that'll help him in a fight. If anything, they expand the bull's-eye Pendon has, for whatever reason, plastered on him.

A few yards away, Cardo and the other Disciples look on. They're curious but not jumping in yet—just letting us know they're ready, they're locked and loaded. I keep looking for Mig, their leader, to come and get his boy, but he's nowhere in sight. Pendon's on his own. He's free-styling. The other Disciples draw closer, form that half circle again. I know what that half circle means: any of you geek turds make a move on our boy, you just declared war on the Disciples of Vice.

Well, they can chill the hell out on that one. If anything is for damn sure, it's that the geeks are not stupid. They're a bunch of pussies. And I mean that with all due respect. If you can't defend yourself with your fists, your weapons, or your posse, being a pussy is basically your best and only defense. All the geeks have to do—and I think they know it—is ride out Pendon's tirade until he runs out of steam.

And they're riding. They're taking it like bitches. It's a perfect performance.

Until Memmo—Mexican, fluent in Spanish—decides to flip the script on the silent treatment. He's only trying to be helpful, providing a little translation service for Salim, who, if he does speak anything besides English, it sure ain't Spanish.

This does not go over well with Pendon. He puts his tirade on hold, takes a breather from Salim and steps straight up into Memmo's business. Memmo's the shortest guy at Haverland, basically the size of a third grader, so now he's looking up at this pissed-off Disciple like one of those babies in a sling, his dumb brown eyes blinking, blinking, blinking, like he's surprised Pendon's mad at him.

"What's going on?" Fitzpatrick mutters.

Shut up! I think to myself. Do these people not know the script? When a pissed-off Disciple of Vice has something to get off his chest, especially one as crazy as Flavio Pendon, you sit tight and leave him to it. You don't go asking for an explanation. But I don't say anything because I am trying to disappear. My plan is to blend right in to the brick wall behind me. If anyone happens to look in my direction, all they'll see is a light brown smear of mud. That's what I'm hoping.

Memmo's in rare form today. He's left his brain in his cell. He actually answers Fitzpatrick's idiot question.

"He says he don't like what Salim wrote in that movie review."

"What?" Fitzpatrick says, his pink face all pinched up. "You mean that review of *Deadpool?* In the newsletter? He actually read it?"

"He says it disrespecting his man."

"But it was a good review," Fitzpatrick says.

Who cares? I want to scream. The problem here isn't some stupid movie review. It's the pissed off Disciple with an army at his back.

"It's 'coz he said it was better than *X-Men,*" Memmo explains. "And *X-Men* his favorite movie."

Just then, Pendon backs away from Memmo to shake his head in disbelief. These two, Memmo and Fitzpatrick, have just inserted themselves into a dispute he had with Salim and Salim alone. Now he's got to figure out what to do about *them.* He scans the geeks until he spots me up against that wall. I hold my hands out in front of me like, *This ain't my fight. I've got nothing to add.* Pendon fumes for a few seconds while he makes up his mind about something. He's got a lot to think about now. The reasons for justifiable, possibly even *necessary,* violence just keep adding up.

This is not the first time I have witnessed this flavor of bullshit, either inside Haverland or out. But that doesn't mean it's predictable. There are all kinds of wild cards. A shiv in the waistband. A signal to the Disciples. A yard-wide riot. It's not choreography we're doing here. It's chaos.

For one blessed moment, it seems like Pendon has run out of ammo. Maybe he's thinking that Salim, Memmo, and Fitzpatrick are such a lowly trio of juvie pussies he doesn't need to waste any more time on them. And his posse is in no hurry to escalate this. They're hanging back, showing their support, but no way are they looking to brawl. Pendon turns to go, and I can feel the relief running through all the geeks.

But then, two paces out, he spins around and drops Salim with a professional-grade right hook.

Salim goes down like a sack of onions.

He doesn't get up either. I can't tell if he's unconscious or faking it. Either scenario is fine as long as it puts an end to this. And it *should* put an end to it. Pendon's said his piece, landed his punch, upped his cred as the baddest dog in the Disciples pack. Surely a knockout punch of that caliber is enough payback for one stupid movie review, right? Nope. This particular Disciple plays by his own rules. And those rules involve raining down more fury in one beat down than most people see in a lifetime.

Deon, Huang, and Little Anthony can't just watch anymore. They start clawing at Pendon's back. The other geeks start circling, like they want to help but they don't know how. I'm still sitting against that wall, trying to blend in. When I stand up, hoping to sneak the hell out of there, I catch Cardo staring at me.

That's when I figure out why he and his friends are standing where they are. They're positioned there to block the view of the guards. Everyone else in the yard read that signal perfectly too. Even the ones who want in hang back.

I do not want in. This is not my fight. I never read that newsletter. I never watched those movies. I've got no opinion on any of this.

Eventually, the guards run over and peel Pendon off of Salim, then march everyone—myself included—to the door. The rest of the Disciples watch us go. Just what they wanted. They played the whole thing perfectly.

CHAPTER 20

Nobody disputes that the fight was instigated by Flavio Pendon, drug dealer, man-slaughterer, and middle ranking Disciple of Vice. The guards do not blame Salim for writing that review or Memmo for volunteering his translation services or even (and I actually disagree with them on this one) Fitzpatrick for trying to talk sense into the guy. Only Pendon gets sent to solitary with a mark on his record that will make a star appearance at his next court date.

This is a mixed blessing, since Pendon will eventually be released from solitary. He'll be in the same cafeteria and, in some cases, the same classes as the geeks. The odds of someone like Flavio Pendon using his stint in solitary to examine his "rage issues" or his demented allegiance to the movie *X-Men* are long. If anything, he'll come out with a chip on his shoulder about the whole thing.

THAT NIGHT I DREAD returning to my cell. Cardo's been back with me for a week now, and it's usually the same routine. He starts off with some kind of insult to let me know we're not friends. Then, after a few minutes of silence, he starts talking at me just like he used to. Cardo can't handle silence. Everything with him is for show—his toughness, his renewed allegiance to the Disciples. It's all part of the act he puts on, the game he's playing.

I have no interest in figuring out the nature of this game. As far as I can tell, his future is fucked. And I can't be sure, but I think he's doing drugs now too. He's jittery all the time. Sometimes he'll jump straight out of his bunk and grind out a hundred push-ups, then bounce around the cell like a caged tiger. Maybe he's taking steroids.

I figure I'll let him lecture me on whatever he thinks I did wrong out in the yard that day, take some unsolicited advice on the best way to deal with psychos like Flavio Pendon, pretend I value his opinion.

The truth is I feel kind of guilty about the whole thing. For better or worse, the geeks are my peeps now and I can't help but wonder if going after Salim was the Disciples' way of making up for the fact that they let me off so easy the other day. They have their reputation as hardasses to think of. Maybe by refusing to be punked out in the yard by Cardo, I wound up putting the geeks at risk. You never know. Thug logic and all. So I ask Cardo if he'll put in a good word with the Disciples for the geeks, tell him none of the geeks have anything personally against Flavio Pendon, the Disciples, or the movie *X-Men*.

But Cardo's not interested in helping me out on this one.

"You just tell your geek pussy friend to watch what he writes," is his advice.

"It was a movie review, Cardo. How's he supposed to know your friend's a fan of *X-Men*?"

"Don't talk to me about how he's supposed to know. It don't matter. He knows now. He pissed my man off. You're saying he got too hot over this? Okay, that's your opinion. But I ain't rushing in to cool him down. They already think I'm too tight with you."

"Fine. Forget I asked."

"And stop asking me for stupid shit." He snorts in disgust. "Put in a *word* for you. Like I'm gonna do that."

I know better than to argue with Cardo on this one. No matter how insane it seems to someone like me, it makes total sense to the Disciples that Flavio Pendon will actually kill a guy over a movie review. And there's not a damn thing anyone can do about that except try to stay out of his way.

CHAPTER 21

In computer class the next day, I have to do a tutorial on spread-sheets, which, according to Stanley Huang, is a great way to keep track of my "finances." And here I was thinking you're just supposed to keep your cash in a doll under your sister's bed. As soon as Huang clears off, I open an email from Janelle.

She found me.

My heart sinks. But I knew this would happen eventually. Karen West is lazy and stupid, but even she has enough marbles to figure out that the best way to track down a *middle schooler* is at the *middle school.* According to Janelle, she showed up drunk and demanded that everybody stop "kidnapping" her daughter. When the principal refused to hand Janelle over that very second, she went full-blown bitch about all the lawyers she was going to hire to "bust everyone up."

I have no trouble picturing this. Anything can set my mother off. An empty booze bottle, the cashier at McDonald's not giving her enough ketchup packets. Her eyes will shrink into angry slits and her skinny lips will disappear into whatever teeth she has left while she unloads a steaming pile of bullshit.

The principal was so impressed with my mother's

performance, she called the Department of Children and Families on her. My mother split before they got there, but the principal had her address. So a nice social worker from DCF had the chance to observe Karen West's beautiful home during a surprise visit. And what an impression she made. The social worker was especially moved by the smell of urine everywhere (not just in the bathroom but "everywhere"). Then there was the food rotting on the counter and the dozens of flies circling the trash can.

Lady says there were maggots on the floor. Maggots! And then Mom fell asleep while she was inspecting the bedroom. I don't even want to know what she found in there.

This is actually good news. The social worker had just enough time before my mother passed out to tell her that Janelle would not be allowed to return home. She would probably lose her daughter to the wonders of foster care if she didn't make some serious changes.

But far be it from Karen West to bow out gracefully—or even to bow out in a puddle of her own puke. No, Karen West is not going to sit by in her house of maggots while Janelle gets "spoilt" by her "cushy," "charmed" existence in some foster home. Screw that, girlfriend. Why should Janelle have all the fun? My mother can rally. She doesn't do it that often. It basically takes someone threatening to "kidnap" her children. But if change is needed to keep Janelle within striking distance, then change it will be. She can clean her house. She can empty the trash. And, more importantly, she can enter rehab.

Ah, rehab.

You know she's only doing it to get me back and it means Mrs. Rodriguez can't get paid for being a foster mom.

*Basically she says I can only stay there until she gets out of
rehab. Then I have to come back home. And the stupid cow
from DCF signs off on this cause a person's supposed to get
a "second chance." Can you believe that? Second chance?
How about, like, five hundred chances. You know how rehab
goes.*

I know exactly how rehab goes. My mother can jump on
and off the wagon like it's barely moving. Rehab is fun. It's
full of people whose job is to listen to her.

*Oh and here's the best part. That lady from DCF got her in
some accelerated detox so she'll be finished when you get out.
I swear to God, Mom manipulated her. I don't know how
'cause she's not that smart or anything, but she must have.*

Actually, DCF probably made that call so they wouldn't
have to find a foster home for me when I get out of juvie.
I don't do so well in foster homes. And finding one for a
sixteen-year-old with a record isn't easy. That lady was just
being practical.

*Anyway, at least you'll be home soon. But Isaac I'm telling
you, the second you turn eighteen, I'm moving out with you.
I don't care what it takes. I can't do this anymore. I'll quit
school and babysit full-time if I have to. But you and me,
we're getting out of here.*

CHAPTER 22

On Monday, Dr. Horton decides to give me a break. We've spent the past week talking about guilt and shame, mostly mine, but everyone shared their own stories too. It was like a greatest hits collection of backstabbing, rage, and stupidity. No surprises there. My story isn't even the worst of them. Everyone in that room is in some stage of "working through it."

The first step is accepting full responsibility for your actions. Until you do that you're "living underground," in Javier's words. Supposedly, this is why I'm so "closed off" and "secretive." You have to find the strength to own what you've done, say it out loud.

In my case that means admitting to myself and everyone in there that I'm just as guilty of putting Mr. Christaldi into that coma as Pat Healy is. The fact that I took the rap for Healy means nothing. It's a legal technicality and it doesn't make up for the fact that I did nothing while my partner beat a man with a rock.

I know they're right. And as hard as it was to come out and say it, I know there's something decent about taking responsibility for what happened that night. It's the kind of thing that can make you a better person if you let it.

I have nothing but respect for what they're doing in here. It's hard work. Sandra struggling to stop disappearing so she can own up to killing D'nesh Patel. Barbie putting herself in the shoes of Enrique Cabron's mother, imagining that woman's grief and owning it. And Javier. He's the bravest of them all, reliving the night he and his brother attacked another kid for the stupidest reason imaginable. The kid insulted his brother's girlfriend. Now he's dead. Javier carries that with him every minute of the day. He never lets up, never gives himself a break. He doesn't disappear like Sandra or go underground like me. He never hides behind a stone-cold game face like Barbie Santiago. He's a killer and he's going to be dragging his victim's corpse around for the rest of his life. I have so much admiration for Javier. I've never met anyone so determined to fight for his own soul.

"So," Dr. Horton says. "Life stories. Did everyone bring one?"

That was the assignment this time. A life story. It could be happy or sad, as long as it mattered. Barbie promised to write a happy story because it was getting too heavy in there. I couldn't agree more. Javier actually wrote a poem. By choice.

It's Riley up now, going on and on about some biology teacher: "So when she asked for a volunteer, Chet Warmley stood up. He didn't even raise his hand, because he's the kind of guy who always gets whatever he wants." Riley clears his throat and, in a high-pitched voice I guess is supposed to sound like his teacher, says, "This is how you do the Heimlich maneuver." He starts giggling like a little girl. "So then she stood behind Chet and put her arms around his stomach to demonstrate. And . . ."

Another fit of giggles. He needs to work on that.

"Then while she explained to the class about the Heimlich maneuver, Chet got a total *boner* right in front of everyone!"

There's a brief pause. Then Wayne tears it open with a laugh like a hyena. Barbie snickers. Even Sandra cracks a smile. The only one who isn't laughing is Javier.

"Dude, why you be telling us a life story about Chet What's-His-Name when you supposed to be telling one 'bout yourself?" Javier says.

"Because." Riley is still caught up in his little girl's squeal. "Everyone laughed at him, but I laughed the hardest, so I was the one he beat on after school. I guess I should have included that part." He leans back and points to a scar under his chin. "He's this big varsity wrestler dude, so I couldn't even really fight back."

"Which would have been fierce though, right?" Barbie says.

"It's impossible to say. He had a definite weight advantage. Anyway, Dr. Horton said we could tell any story we wanted."

Javier shrugs. He doesn't care for Riley's boner story.

Wayne likes it though. He taps his temple. "Excellent story, my man. I'm keeping that one for later. And this dude beat you up?"

Riley nods.

"'Coz he humiliated, that's why. And he taking it out on somebody else, like *you* the one humiliated him."

"Well I did laugh *really* loud. I mean, like, louder than anyone. I don't think I've ever laughed that loud in my life. I was out of control."

Wayne shakes his head at this. "Damn, Riles. You one strange MF, you know that?"

Riley stares back, wounded.

There's some weird chemistry between those two. I can't put my finger on it. It doesn't seem possible that they knew each other outside of juvie, but inside it's definitely a love-hate thing.

"Anyway," Dr. Horton says. "It's not about breaking down these stories today. It's about sharing. Thanks, Riley. Who's next? Javier? Do you have a poem for us?"

"It's not my best."

"It's okay. We're not grading anything."

"Yeah," Wayne says. "It'll still be better than anything *we* write. My story sucked."

"No it didn't," Javier says. "It was honest, man. That's what matters. Just like Dr. Horton says. This is all about how honest we can be. 'Coz that takes courage. But sometimes . . ." Javier shakes his head. "I don't know, man. I'm not sure I'm *being* so honest when I write in this thing. Like I be working so hard to make the words right instead of just saying how it is. I feel like I *know* your brother, Wayne, and how he tried to shake those drugs. Don't need no fancy words for that, no rhyming or shit. Damn, Wayne, you the best writer in here."

Technically, it's a compliment. But Wayne looks like he's just been slapped.

"Well *I* want to hear your poem," Barbie says. "I think we were promised a poem, right Dr. Horton? So you ain't gettin' out of it that easy."

"For what it's worth," Dr. Horton says, "I have the one you typed out for me framed in my office at home."

"Really?"

"Read it!" Barbie taunts.

Man, these guys sure love poetry.

"Yeah, come on, man," Wayne says. "But you got to read it twice, 'coz I only understand your poems the second time."

"Poetry's like that," Javier says. "You got to work for it."

"And we ready to work," Barbie says. "So lay that mofo down."

Javier's torn. He wants to share his poem. But something's holding him back.

"I've never heard your poetry," I tell him. "Hell, I don't think I've ever heard poetry. Not out loud, anyway. You gonna deprive me of my rightful education? Man, that's cold."

"The boy's right," Barbie says. She even smiles at me, maybe the first time I've ever been on the receiving end of a legit smile from Barbie Santiago. I have to fight to keep from smiling back like an idiot.

"All right, all right. But this a work in progress. I ain't even sure what I'm trying to say yet."

"Just say it slow," Wayne says. "So we can keep up."

Javier takes a breath, then opens his notebook and begins.

> *I don't deserve this.*
> *The stink, the food.*
> *Somebody always watching.*
> *Somebody always judging.*
> *Claustrophobia. I looked it up in class.*
> *Walls closing in,*
> *I don't deserve that.*
> *Some fool charge me up.*
> *Some punk hit me up.*
> *Guards mistrusting*
> *Cellie always fussing.*
> *Dirty windows*
> *we can't see out.*
> *Lights out, ladies*
> *Lights up, ladies.*
> *Do this. Go there.*
> *I don't deserve this.*
> *Lawyer don't know shit.*
> *Judge don't give a shit.*
> *Lock him up, shut him up.*
> *I don't deserve this.*
> *I ain't no king.*
> *I ain't no disciple.*
> *Why you be spending your taxes on me?*
> *I'm not some kid needs a second chance.*
> *I'm not some kid. Ain't been one for years.*

I'm your nightmare come true.
You don't wake up from this.
The stink, the food.
The dirty windows.
Walls closing in.
Walls closing in.
I don't deserve this.
It's too good for me.

Javier pauses for a second then leans back in his chair.

Nobody moves or says anything.

"Again?" Dr. Horton says.

Javier nods then rereads it. The second time through, he lets his emotions come out, like he's feeling it all for real. Right there, in the room with us. I'm feeling it too. When he gets to the last line, it shocks me, even though I've already heard it.

"Damn, Jav," Barbie says. "You set that to a beat and you be up there with the masters."

"It ain't a rap," Javier says. "Rappers be selling their lifestyles and how they all bad and shit. This ain't about that."

"Yeah, but you could tell it *your* way," Barbie says. "Just use them millionaire record companies to get the word out."

Wayne nods.

"I have to agree with Barbie," Riley says. "It's a shame to have all that talent and just waste it."

Even Sandra offers up a quiet "Yup."

Javier shakes his head. "I ain't wasting it. I'm giving it to you."

"That's wasting it," Wayne says. "You should have a bigger audience."

"I don't want an audience. It ain't about that."

"So what's it about?" I ask. "I mean the rest of us just write down what happened."

"That's what I'm doing too."

Now I'm the one shaking my head. I can't explain why, but there's something more to Javier's poem than to Riley's or Wayne's stories. Something about the rhythm and the language makes it deeper, like he's inviting us all in.

"Have you ever thought about trying to get your poems published?" Dr. Horton asks.

"Like what? In the newspaper or something?"

"Or in a literary journal."

The words don't mean much to Javier.

"We should have an open mic!" Barbie says. "Like in them clubs when they let people come up and do their raps."

"It's a poem not a rap," Javier reminds her.

"And then the audience votes on who's best by making a lot of noise."

"My stupid cellmate will get up there, no doubt," Riley says. "He never shuts up. He's always rhyming everything. Like yesterday I said, 'Where's my toothbrush,' and he goes, 'You get smoove crush.' What's that supposed to mean?"

"Dr. Horton," Barbie says. "How come we can't have something like that in here? Don't you agree it would be good for self-esteem and confidence and shit? And then the girls can have a dance contest."

"Barbie, that's precisely why we can't do something like that," Dr. Horton explains calmly. "Every time you girls practice your dance moves out in the yard, some boy on cafeteria duty gets sent to solitary."

"That's 'coz a girl's body her best weapon." Barbie stands up and jams those deadly curves into a body roll. "Ain't that right, Sandra?" She tosses the girl a wink, then sits down and crosses her ankle over her knee.

"All right, all right," Dr. Horton says. "This isn't *American Idol.*"

Barbie's little dance party is over quickly, but it's enough to convince me to get myself on cafeteria duty *by any means necessary.* I'll gladly take a stint in solitary for the chance to see that move again. I'm still seeing it now. I have a feeling I'll be seeing it all night.

"What's a literary magazine?" Javier asks suddenly.

"It's um . . . You know what? We'll talk later. Who's next? Isaac? You want to go?"

My stomach flips over. "All right, well mine's about the worst day of my life."

"Awesome," Riley says. He might mean it sarcastically, but with Riley you can't always tell. And anyway, in the orange-rug room, stories like mine actually count as gifts. Believe it or not, this is the kind of crap we give each other. I open my notebook and start to read.

This happened about three years ago. I was thirteen and my sister, Janelle, was ten. We were living in this one-bedroom shelter in Ashland with my mom. Usually, my mom would send my sister and me out into the hallway when one of her customers came, but there was this junkie who was lying around out there, so she told us to just sit on the couch and watch TV. But she forgot that we didn't have a cable box. All we could do was watch our own reflections and make stupid faces at each other, like pig noses and fish mouths.

The guy was really loud in her bedroom. We could hear my mom complaining about it, like he was hurting her or something. So I got up to go check on her, but my sister grabbed my hand and told me to stay right there because she was scared. She had these sharp nails that dug into my skin. I didn't want to leave her alone, so we just sat there holding hands. We weren't looking at the TV anymore though. We were looking over the back of the couch at the bedroom door, which was stupid because the door was closed, so we couldn't see anything.

The guy kept getting louder and my Mom was yelling at him. I wanted to go help her, but every time I tried to get up, my sister would squeeze my hand and dig her nails into it, saying, "Stay with me. Stay with me." She was so scared. And I realized that I had to protect her, not my mom. I couldn't protect both of them at the same time. So I stayed with my sister, even when my mom started crying. The guy was in there for fourteen minutes, which I counted on the broken DVD player.

Then he came out of the bedroom, and my sister and me hid between the couch and a cardboard box on the floor that was like a coffee table. But he saw us when he got to the door. He didn't say anything though. He just left.

When I close the notebook, everyone's staring at me. But it's different this time. They believe me.

"So your mom's, like, a . . ." Riley can't finish that sentence.

"She's a prostitute. Yeah."

It's the first time I've ever said that word out loud. I won't say it feels good, but at least I feel safe saying it. I don't feel the need to punch Riley's lights out for bringing it up.

"She still in the life?" Barbie asks.

I nod.

"Drugs?"

"Gin."

"Old school."

Everyone's quiet. But it's not a mean quiet. They're not judging me or my mother. It's something else. It's like they're creating space around my story, leaving me room to feel something about it, letting me know it's okay to feel something about it too, even in front of them. We're *supposed* to feel things in here. That's the idea. That's why I brought them this story. You might think you're protecting your-self by shutting down your feelings, but all you're doing is sending them underground. And an underground feeling is much more dangerous because it's out of your control. That's what they say, and I get that now.

These people all come here to the orange-rug room for the same reason I came: because a judge told them to. But you don't make it here if you're just ticking off a box. You come in here like I did, full of bullshit and attitude, you'll wash out in a week. The ones who survive are the ones who put it all on the line. Like Javier. He doesn't hide anything. Whatever he's got, he's sharing. These people show up every day for each other because they know. You try to face some-thing like Ashland on your own, or something like what Sandra did to D'nesh Patel, it will swallow you up.

"Thanks, Isaac," Dr. Horton says. "I think that leaves Barbie."

"Here we go," Wayne says with a roll of his eyes.

Barbie makes a big show of setting herself up to read. She presses her legs together like a lady and straightens up real proper. "Prepare to be blown away."

I'm relieved when everyone stops looking at me. Dr. Horton looks over to see if I'm okay and I nod. I *am* okay, but only because I'll never have to tell that story again. I'm proud of myself for sharing it. They deserve it. Nothing but the worst for your teammates. But I'm glad it's over now. When I get back to my cell, I'm going to tear that page out of my notebook and put Ashland behind me once and for all.

Barbie tells the story of her quinceañera, the big party Latinas get when they turn fifteen. I can't quite imagine her in the yellow puffy dress she describes. When she's not in juvie scrubs, I picture her in full-on ghetto wear—baggy jeans, wifebeater. Butch, but smoking hot.

Everyone was making a big deal about the chambelanes and how my date was all jealous of everyone, but all I cared about was they had found my old friend, Mariana, and when was she going to get there.

Mariana was my girl. I couldn't wait to see her and find out what she been up to the last year since she moved to LA. We were tight. But it was nine o'clock and no Mariana, then it was ten o'clock and still no Mariana. Then they be closing the hall down and everyone leaving and, finally, I see someone sitting on the stairs outside by the entrance.

She's wearing a short skirt and these nasty sneakers and some kind of sweatshirt with holes in it. She all skinny and hunched over, but I recognize that hair, 'coz Mariana had this wild hair like a tumbleweed.

And I run up to her and I say, "Hey, chica, why you sitting out here when the party's inside?" And she look all sad and telling me she embarrassed because she can't afford a nice dress and we all flash in our ballgowns and tuxedoes. I'm wearing a tiara so I look like the Queen of England or something, but hot. So I make a joke about how it's all fake and I wouldn't ever dress like that except for my quinceañera. Then I tell her how it don't matter what she's wearing 'coz I'm just happy to finally see her.

But she won't even get up to give me a hug. It's like she stuck there or something. So I sit down next to her and that's when I notice her arms. They all tracked up. She real skinny and she dressed like a ho. And it all makes sense now. She is a ho, and a junkie too. I would have seen that right away except she was my girl and you know how you always see the best when you love someone.

Then she tells me she ain't even been to LA. She been in Worcester this whole time, like an hour away. And all that year, while I been living it up, running the town, and planning my quinceañera, she be trickin' for some pimp in Worcester. Her mom's dead and her dad beats her all the time. She sleepin' in cars and shit. Then she asks me for money and I know it's to buy drugs and I'm thinking no way, this my chica. This Mariana. I want to take her home, get her cleaned up and shit, so I stick my tiara on her head and go inside to tell my mom she's coming home with us that night.

But when I come back out, she gone. My cousin said she walked off. I made him drive me all over, but we couldn't find her. I kept asking everybody for days if they seen her, but she just vanished. My other cousin, the one who tracked her down in the first place, said the phone number she got was dead. That was the last time I saw Mariana. She kept the tiara, which was a rental, so my Mom got mad about that. But I didn't care. I hope she didn't sell it though. I hope she's keeping it safe somewhere and taking it out once in a while to think of me. 'Coz even though she a ho and a junkie, she still my girl.

When she's finished, Barbie snaps the notebook shut and falls back into her chair, satisfied.

"I thought you were readin' a happy story," Wayne says.

"I *was* happy when my cousin told me she found Mariana."

"What do you think happened to her?" Riley asks.

"Either she dead by now, or she still trickin'. 'Coz if she not trickin' I know she'd come looking for me."

"How do you know?" Javier asks. "She only a hour away that whole time and she don't call you?"

"'Coz she in the life," Barbie says. "Ask Sandra. She knows how it is. They cut you off from your friends, make you think they your enemies, like they going to deprive you of a living or something. That night at my quinceañera, she wasn't even Mariana anymore. She like some dead girl walking around. So either she really dead now or she'll find her way back."

Back to what? I wonder. Back to Barbie's neighborhood, where Barbie doesn't live anymore? Even if Barbie wasn't locked up in juvie, what could she do to help Mariana? Jump her into a gang? For some girls, that means basically getting gang raped.

"Shit, Barbie," Wayne says. "I thought I'd be leaving here with some kind of positivity. Now all's I got is Riley's boner story and a bunch of sad shit to add to my own."

"Yeah, Barbie," Riley says. "I hate to say it, but you kind of let us down."

"You guys were really counting on me?" she asks, like she's touched by it.

Wayne shakes his head. "It's like you said. It's getting too heavy in here. Sometimes . . . I don't know, man. Sometimes I start wondering what's the point."

"You can't think like that, Wayne," Riley says. "That's letting defeat win."

"No, Wayne's right," Javier says. "This about being honest, right, Dr. Horton?"

Dr. Horton nods.

"And if we honest, we got to admit some of us ain't going to make it. Like that girl Mariana? I'm sorry to be the one to say this, Barbie, and you know I praying for that girl tonight."

Barbie taps her chest with her fist in thanks.

"But you know she ain't coming out of that," Javier continues. "Unless there some miracle. And Sandra's father? He ain't never gonna be a real father to her. And Isaac's mom? The booze *her* best friend. She ain't giving that up."

"Unless there's some miracle," I say.

"But we don't live in a world of miracles," Javier says. "You see water turning into wine anywhere? Or dudes walking on water?"

"This ain't helpin'," Wayne says.

"But we got to face it. Because if we relying on some miracle to save us, we all doomed."

Just then Sandra mutters something. When Dr. Horton asks her to repeat it, she shakes her head and says, "Nothing."

"It's not nothing, Sandra," he says. "If you said it, it counts."

This only frightens her, drives her even further behind those knees. Sandra never volunteers to say anything. She has to be coaxed. Nobody says anything. By now even I know the drill. If Dr. Horton asks Sandra to speak, we have to wait for her to speak. There's no taking the fifth in group.

Eventually she says, "We can be our own miracle."

Wayne sighs. "That's a nice thought, Sandra, but I ain't got that kind of confidence in myself. I'm not saying I'm all bad. I know I got some good qualities. But I ain't being my own *miracle*."

"What about being someone else's?" Dr. Horton asks.

"Yeah," Sandra says. "That's what I meant."

"How's that supposed to work?" Wayne asks.

Sandra looks at Barbie. "Is it okay if I tell them?"

Barbie turns to Dr. Horton. "This here's confidential, right?"

Dr. Horton looks worried.

"So I can't get in trouble for anything that gets said here, right?"

"Barbie?"

"I'm just asking if it's confidential?" Barbie insists. "You said that, right?"

He nods, his face grim. "Yes. It's confidential."

"I'm only bending the rules anyway. I ain't hurting nobody."

Dr. Horton looks like he's one more question away from losing his temper. "Go on, Sandra. Tell us what Barbie did."

"Well, Barbie's been helping me track down my father."

Dr. Horton's eyes flash.

"Not so she can *see* him," Barbie says.

"Yeah, I don't ever want to see him again," Sandra agrees.

"That's good, Sandra," Riley says. "That's progress. Right, Dr. Horton?"

Riley hates tension. He's always trying to defuse it, make peace, find common ground.

But Dr. Horton isn't ready for peace yet. "What exactly do you mean by *tracking him down?*"

I can understand his concern. Barbie's a killer. She's also a member of Sol Dominicano. These people do not "track people down" to invite them over for a barbecue.

"It's so Sandra can warn his new kids," Barbie says. "See, he remarried to some lady with three kids her own and Sandra wants to make sure they know what they getting into."

"Two girls and a boy," Sandra says. "That's all I know. And that they move around a lot. Like we used to."

"So I got some of those computer dudes to help me do a search on him. Only he change his name a lot, so it's not so easy."

"What computer dudes?" Dr. Horton asks.

"Aw come on, man. They're not doing anything wrong. We just trying to help those kids and help Sandra get closure on her dad."

"That's not closure," Dr. Horton says.

"But she can't erase what he already done to her," Barbie says, her voice rising. "So she just trying to prevent him from doing it to somebody else. What's wrong with that?"

"A lot." Dr. Horton doesn't raise his voice. His anger is cool, under control. "We can't have you approaching people on the outside, Barbie. That's extremely dangerous. Sandra, I want to meet with your counselor to talk about this."

Sandra looks petrified.

"But Sandra's counselor's a dude," Barbie spits. "Like you

a dude. I don't mean no disrespect, Dr. Horton, but how you supposed to understand this?"

"Barbie—"

"You can't. No way a dude gets this. But I been there. I'm the only one in here who understands what Sandra's been through. Ain't none of you understand it." She dismisses all of us in one sweeping glance. "You got to have this body—a *girl's* body—to know what that kind of vulnerability all about. You telling me you know that, Dr. Horton? Shit, you like seven foot tall. You don't know what vulnerable is till you had some dude bearing down on you and it don't matter what you want. Ask Sandra. Ask Isaac's mother. There's certain things you can *never* understand. And you better thank your lucky stars for it too. I'm only tryin' to help."

"We'll talk afterwards," Dr. Horton says.

"You bustin' me?" Barbie's tone is hostile now, threatening.

I imagine a horrible chain of events—a phone call, an order for a tail—all of it ending with a revenge hit on Dr. Horton.

But Dr. Horton shakes his head. "I'm not busting anyone. But I'd like to know what you plan to do when you find him."

"We gonna contact his new wife and kids," Barbie says.

"How?"

"Email."

Dr. Horton shakes his head. "We'll talk afterwards. Sandra, if you want to request a female counselor, if you think that would help—"

"I just want to stop him before he hurts those kids," Sandra says. "Those kids are innocent."

Not for long, I think. If her father isn't stopped—and honestly? he won't be—his new kids are already on their way toward the Boulevard of Bad Fathers. And that's assuming they aren't already living there.

"Dr. Horton," Javier says. "For what it's worth, I think this a worthwhile project. Maybe Barbie should have talked to you first, but seriously, she's just trying to help."

"And Sandra too," Wayne adds.

Dr. Horton doesn't answer right away. He's obviously upset with Barbie for starting this project without his permission. But what can he honestly say? Is anyone, besides Barbie and Sandra, looking out for those kids? DCF? Their mother? Their mother invited that monster into her home, and DCF *never* steps in until the shit's already gone down.

"I'll want to meet with these computer guys," Dr. Horton says. "And don't worry. I'm not busting anyone. But I want to make sure Sandra's not endangering herself in any way. You either, Barbie." He takes a deep breath. "You showed initiative. Both of you. And that's great. I applaud that. But I need you to understand that there are adults here who can help you. You've got to reach out to us."

"Mr. Klein's an adult," Barbie says.

"Who's Mr. Klein?"

"He's the teacher in the computer room."

"Is he the one who's helping you?"

Barbie nods.

"Anyone else?"

Barbie hesitates, then shakes her head. "No, just Klein."

For a split second, I'm tempted to bust Stanley Huang. I've seen him sniffing around Barbie plenty of times. Now I know why. How come he gets to be Barbie's hero?

"So, Barbie's doing this for Sandra," Riley says. "Sandra, what are you doing for Barbie?"

"Nothing," Barbie says. "Can't a girl do something for another girl without it being for profit?"

"She's being my miracle," Sandra says.

"That's right. I'm being Sandra's miracle."

"I'd be hers, too, if I knew how," Sandra says. Then she sinks back behind her knees.

"Maybe you can be someone else's miracle," Riley says.

"Whose?"

"You can be mine."

"Okay. How?"

"Um . . ." Riley's eyes roll up to the ceiling. "I'll get back to you."

"So, who gonna be my miracle?" Wayne asks.

"Not me," Barbie says. "I'm tapped out. What about you, Javier?"

Javier nods. "You know I'm there for you, man."

"Sure," Wayne says. "You there and all, but how's that supposed to be a miracle? I'm talking results, man. Like Barbie delivering for Sandra."

"Well, what you need?" Javier asks.

After that, they all start arguing about the difference between miracles versus just "helping out." I have my doubts about the whole thing. Maybe Barbie will be able to track that guy down and warn his new wife. But who's to say she'll even listen. Barbie's a criminal. We all are.

Just then I have an idea.

"Javier," I whisper because I don't want the others in on it. "You really want to get your poem published?"

"Yeah. Why?"

"Make me a copy. Right now."

Javier stares at me for a second, then takes out his pen and copies his poem. "What you up to?"

"Just trying to be someone's miracle."

When he hands it over, I can tell he half believes me.

CHAPTER 23

For the record, I don't actually believe in miracles. The idea of some supernatural force working outside the usual flip-flop of good and bad luck is for other people—people who can afford Sunday clothes, people whose relatives give them gold crosses to wear around their necks, like the pretty Italian girls at Holy Name Girls Academy. I just want to do something for Javier. As far as I'm concerned, the only thing that would qualify as a miracle would be if my mom gets out of rehab and stays sober for more than three weeks. If that happens, I'll believe in anything.

Deon's late to the computer room. Barbie's there, working with Huang. So I hold on to Javier's poem and get to work on a spreadsheet tutorial that Huang has set up for me. It's my eleventh day in computer class, and I'm getting the hang of it. The computer's not a stupid box trying to mess with me anymore. It's a tool. It works for me. I don't even need Huang anymore. Whatever I need to know, I can find it in one of those help menus or search windows. If only life were like that.

search: *ways to get my mother off my sister's case*
search: *ways to escape from juvie without winding up in jail.*

My email inbox is constantly tugging at me, but I've worked out a system with Janelle. To avoid breaking the rule about reading emails before doing work, I told her to use long descriptions in the subject line. That way I can quickly scan my inbox to make sure she's okay. Today there are three emails from her with the subject lines: *I'm playing volleyball again!*, *Daniela's baby brother is sooooo cute*, and *Everything's cool but I still hate Mom*. These I can leave until later, when I've mastered the all-important skill of spreadsheets.

What the hell am I going to do with spreadsheets?

Every day there are more and more emails from strangers. I know it's all spam. Janelle's the only one with my address. But I open every single one hoping (and believe me, I know how stupid this is) that one of them might be from my father. The only thing I know about him (besides how he walked out on us) is his name: Christopher West. I've already Googled that a million times over. Nothing. Once, my mother told me that West wasn't even his real last name. She also told me once that my father was from Jamaica. Of course, she was wasted both times, so who knows? I Googled "Chris from Jamaica," and you can guess how that went. Unless my dad really is the rapper Chris Brown who performed in Jamaica once, I'm not finding the guy online. Just to be sure, I did the math on Chris Brown's birth date to rule it out.

Most likely my father is also not Christopher Coke, the Jamaican drug lord and leader of the notorious Shower Posse. But he's around the right age. I've spent a lot of time on Christopher Coke's Wikipedia page, trying to see if there's any resemblance. Yeah, I know how messed up it is to *hope* your dad is a Jamaican drug lord. It doesn't stop me though.

When Deon finally shows up, he practically throws himself into his chair. "I hate my lawyer."

"Who doesn't? Hey, I wanted to show you something." I give him Javier's poem.

"What's this?"

"It's a poem."

"So?"

"So what about putting it in *The Free*?"

Barbie looks over at the two of us.

"We don't print poems," Deon says. "It's a newsletter. It's got *news* in it."

"I just thought, I don't know. Maybe liven it up."

"So you think my newsletter needs livening up?"

Smelling controversy, Barbie butts in. "Hey, you know what you should have in that thing? An advice column, where people can ask, like, what should I do if I'm talking to some dude and it's all innocent but then my man sees it and thinks I'm messing around?"

"Yeah, and who's gonna answer?" Deon asks. "You?"

"Why not. Girls asking me stuff all the time. It's like Dear Abby in my cell sometimes."

"I think that's an awesome idea," I say.

"Yeah, me too." Huang. Sad. Trying to angle his way in on the conversation. When no one answers him, he shrinks back and rubs his nose. It's a nervous habit that makes the thing shine like a ruby.

Deon sulks. Not only is his lawyer screwing him over, now everyone's dogpiling on his newsletter.

"Or whatever," I tell him. "It's your thing. It's just that I told this guy I'd help him get published, and I thought, you know, since his poem is all about what it's like being stuck in juvie, maybe people would like it."

"Yeah," Barbie says. "And maybe folks'll actually read the thing."

"They read it," Deon says.

"How many?" she asks. "Honestly, Deon, you working yourself sick on this thing and what two, three people even read it?"

"Flavio Pendon read it."

"Okay that's one." Barbie sticks up her thumb. "All I'm saying is, it's your newsletter sure, but in a for real newspaper there's more than one guy writing stuff."

"I've got other people. I've got Salim's movie reviews. I've got Huang's gaming reviews."

"That's all really great," I say. "But we can't even watch movies in here except the lame shit they show on Wednesday nights. And I don't know about you, but I don't know too many guys in here who have an Xbox. Maybe that's just me and the projects where I live, but . . ."

"You should totally print Javier's rap," Barbie says.

"It's a poem," I remind her. "Not a rap."

"Whatever. You should print it. It's beautiful. Almost made me cry."

Everyone within earshot looks up at this.

She looks around with a scowl. "What? You think I don't got tears? You think I'm some heartless bitch?"

"Isn't that what you want us to think?" Deon asks.

The conversation draws the attention of Mr. Klein. "Is there some work going on over there?"

"Yo, Mr. Klein," Barbie says. "We were just having a discussion on how to make *The Free* more relevant to the folks supposed to be reading it. Isaac thinks we should print this awesome rap—I mean poem—by my boy Javier Muñoz. And I think we should have an advice column for girls."

Mr. Klein nods politely. "What do you think, D?"

Deon looks miserable, but that probably has less to do with the newsletter than with his stupid lawyer. "All right," he says. "But Barbie you got to step up on this. You got to actually answer the questions and type them out."

She smirks. "I got no problem with that."

"And you have to make sure girls actually see this thing."

"I'll pass it out at lunchtime. Make sure every girl gets one. And reads it too."

"And you, Isaac, you're typing up that poem and formatting it."

"I can do that," I lie. I don't know anything about formatting.

"And you better use the spell-checker too," Deon says. "'Coz you spell like a damn second grader."

"I'm sure Stanley was just getting around to teaching me that."

Huang rolls his eyes.

"All good?" Mr. Klein asks Deon.

"Yeah, we're good."

Deon's still miserable, but he doesn't want to talk about it. He wants to hate his lawyer in private. I leave him to it. Sometimes it's easier to get the hate out on your own.

CHAPTER 24

I eat with the geeks now. They're my posse. No one else has to worry about adopting me. I picture a huge sigh of relief from every black guy in the cafeteria. They're not bad as far as geeks go. Smart. Weird. The Cecil Boone incident is behind me, so is that business with Flavio Pendon. Cardo and the Disciples are keeping their distance. I feel almost safe. As safe as you can feel in a place where a stabbing or riot can break out any second.

At the exit of the kitchen near the water dispenser is a cardboard box stuffed with copies of *The Free*. Not that you'd notice. That box has always been there, and I never even saw the thing.

"It needs pictures," I tell Deon. "A big picture of something right on the front page."

Everyone walking by the box ignores it, except for one guy who wipes a booger across the top copy.

"Aw, man," Deon says.

"Well, how you supposed to know what it is? It's just a box. Why don't you at least have a sign on it that says 'Free newsletter. Take one.'"

Huang shakes his head, his cheeks bursting with food. "That's the last thing you'd want. Trust me."

"Why?" I ask.

"They only have a newsletter to get extra funding for the

computer room. It's some journalism grant Klein found. Plus it'll look good on your résumé."

Résumé. Another stupid word. Thanks to Huang and the rules of the computer room, I'll be leaving Haverland with a truckload of skills so pointless they might as well include lion taming and yodeling.

"It's supposed to be available to everyone," Huang says. "But seriously? The last thing you want is for these guys to read *The Free.*"

"Why?" Deon asks.

"You really have to ask?"

"Yeah, I have to ask. What the hell am I working on this thing for if nobody's supposed to read it?"

Everyone tenses up. They're all Huang worshippers. No one ever criticizes him.

"You saying there's no point?" Deon asks. "Because everyone in here a bunch of illiterate negroes and spics?"

"No. I don't think that. Do you?"

"So what am I wasting my time for?"

"Yeah," I say. I'm mad for Deon's sake, but for my own too. I took the time to type out Javier's poem and format it. I had to learn how to use the spell-checker, for crying out loud. But now that I've joined Deon, the argument is breaking down along race lines, and that's not good for anyone. Haverland is always on the lookout for an excuse to pit black against white or brown or yellow. Any bullshit reason will do, even a newsletter nobody reads. So I back off a little. "Seems like a waste of Deon's talent, don't you think? Did you read his article about programmers?"

I myself tried to read it the night before but failed. I'm not a great reader. If something is boring to me—and basically everything written down *is* boring to me—it feels like a thousand knives stabbing me in the face.

"Yeah, right," Huang says. "You want them reading *that*? An article about how geeks discriminate against blacks? We've already got the Disciples on our case, Deon. What do you want now? Bank Street?"

Bank Street's Cecil Boone's gang, an all-black outfit from Dorchester. They're not as psychotic as the Disciples, but you don't want to go pissing them off.

"It's not about how geeks discriminate against blacks," Deon says. "You obviously didn't read it."

"Yeah, I did," Huang says. "But come on, Deon. You have to admit that the main theme—the one that'll get scrawled in the bathroom before someone does a hit on one of us— is that geeks are keeping the black man down. How many people in here you think are gonna read the whole thing?"

Screw Huang for being right. I only got through the first few paragraphs of Deon's article last night, something about how white and Asian programmers are helping each other get ahead while blacks are falling behind. Like, what else is new. It never occurred to me that there was more to it than plain old racism. I'd never start a race war over it, but a lot of guys would.

Now Deon's pissed. He stands up and walks over to the cardboard box with his newsletters in it. Then he roams from table to table, leaving a stack of newsletters on each one. This does not go over well. Folks do not appreciate you coming around to their lunch table and giving them shit to read. They want to read something, they can go to the library on their own. Which they don't.

Eventually, Deon sits down and starts carving up his slab of gray meat without looking at anyone. For better or worse now, everyone has a copy of *The Free*. Some guys are laughing about it, tearing the thing up. One guy on the other side of the cafeteria crumples it up real tight and fires it at our table.

Huang is furious and all the other geeks are scared. Fitzpatrick, the redhead, is actually shaking. He's already paler than snow. Now he's practically see-through.

It was selfish of Deon to act out like that, but I get why he did it. He worked hard on that newsletter. All those little pie charts and graphs. All the footnotes and citations. I don't know what a citation is, but it seems like a lot of work. *The Free* isn't some pointless hobby to Deon. And it isn't just something to put on a résumé either. It probably boils Deon that Mr. Klein never told him it was all some scam to get more money for the computer room. It boils me too. Did he think we were both too thick to understand? Mr. Klein's a racist. So's Huang. I'm sure of it. And when the fighting breaks out, no way am I standing with the geeks. I'm with Deon on this.

I look for the exits and map out a route that will avoid the most dangerous tables—the Disciples, Bank Street, Sol D. I wonder if Cardo will come after me when jungle law breaks out. The Disciples of Vice are not famous for *avoiding* violence.

As the seconds tick by, it gets real quiet. But when I look around, I can't believe what I'm seeing. I elbow Deon, but Deon refuses to look up. He's still filing away at that meat, stuffing it down like it's punishment.

"They're reading it," I whisper.

That gets Deon's attention.

Across the cafeteria, groups of guys are huddling around their copy or grabbing it from each other to read it themselves. Even Cardo and the Disciples are reading it. It gets so quiet in there, it's almost like a library. The guards figure that's not right, so they come out of the kitchen to see what's up.

"We're dead," Fitzpatrick mutters.

If he's right, then death is coming our way in the form of a stumpy, cornrowed hard case with his pants below his butt.

One hand in the waistband, the other one plucking at the vee of his collar, he's the kind of runty kid who actually bigs himself with his shortness, like he has something to prove to the world.

I scan for a weapon. Is it in the waistband? Taped to his stomach?

"Yo, Wilson," the kid says, revealing not one, but three gold teeth.

Deon faces him, scared but cool.

"How come only the girls get to ax Barbie Santiago they questions?" The kid glances around the cafeteria, then raises both of his hands. "Says they getting a box to put they questions in to be anonymous. So where's our box? 'Coz I got a question for Barbie Santiago."

"Me too!" someone yells out.

Deon faces me, like I have the answer. Hard pass on that one, bro. I'm not answering shit. If you asked me right now who Isaac West was, I'd deny the existence of my own self. Isaac? Isaac who? Sorry, never heard of the guy.

Luckily, Deon has a gift for staying cool, even when he's scared shitless. "No problem," he says. Then he strolls over to that water dispenser and holds the empty box over his head. "Put your questions for Barbie Santiago in here," he says to the *whole* cafeteria. Nuts the size of New England, this guy.

A guard comes over to hassle him, but when Deon explains what he's doing and shows him a copy of *The Free*, the guard lets it go. He has a laugh about it with another guard. I guess the idea of a bunch of criminals writing stuff is comedy gold to them. Not to Deon, though. He takes his sweet time walking back to the geek table, drops some swagger into it, like he's a star now and he's going to lap that shit up while he can.

Huang is beside himself. He keeps scanning the room like

he *knows* the hail of bullets is on its way. "If this goes wrong, it's on you, Deon."

"Yeah, yeah," Deon tells him.

It gets loud again, back to its normal state. There's a group of guys reading Javier's poem, pointing it out to their friends, repeating lines out loud. Across the cafeteria, a group of Latinos fake-punch Javier. He looks embarrassed by their attention. When he spots me, he looks down. I can't tell if he's embarrassed or proud. It's one thing to get mad personal in group. It's something else to do it in front of these thugs. I hope I did the right thing. But even if I didn't, it's too late to take it back. That poem is out there. And if the lines bouncing around the cafeteria, backed by improvised mouth beats, are any indication, it's the hit of *The Free*. Like it or not, Javier is a rap star. And I made it happen. Me. Isaac West.

Miracle? Maybe not. But it feels good. When Javier catches my eye, he taps his fist to his chest. No one has ever done that to me before.

CHAPTER 25

"Yo, why you be printing a rap by that ponketo Javier Muñoz anyway?" Cardo asks me that night in our cell. "I see your name on this thing."

He shakes his copy of the newsletter in my face.

"It's not a rap, Cardo. It's a poem."

"It's bullshit. All that crap about 'I don't deserve this.' Fuck you, man. You don't deserve it, then why you sitting here in juvie?"

I've been sitting on my bunk, minding my own beeswax, trying to get through Deon's article about programmers, with many, many breaks to stare into space. It's actually a relief to have an excuse to put it down. "Did you get to the last line?" I ask him.

"Yeah, so what?"

"So what he's saying is he doesn't deserve this because he deserves even worse. It's about feeling worthless, man. Don't you get it? It's about how everything in here is crap and how hard it is, with people telling you what to do and where to go. But that ain't nothing, because deep down you know you don't even deserve *that*. You deserve even harsher things because of what you done."

Cardo's face goes through a series of expressions—disbelief, confusion, ridicule—before settling down into warning.

"So how come you printing this dude's thing, but not something by the Disciples?"

"I didn't know the Disciples of Vice wrote poems."

"You think we can't write this shit? You ever heard Felipe rhyme? That dude rap like nobody's business."

"Yeah, but it's not a rap, Cardo. It's a *poem*."

"What's the difference? 'Cept that punkass Muñoz piece of shit don't even rhyme."

I actually wondered about that myself. But it didn't bother me. Even without rhyming, there's a rhythm to Javier's poem, something musical.

"Look," I say. "If you want to submit something by the Disciples—"

"Hold on. I got to *submit* something? Like, you in charge?"

"I'm not in charge. I just typed out that poem. The newsletter's Deon's thing."

"Deon? You mean Deon Wilson? Dude's a punk."

Everyone's a punk to Cardo now, everyone who isn't Cardo or a member of the Disciples.

"He's all right," I tell him. Saying anything more is a risk not only to my own safety but to Deon's too. I don't know if Deon's all right. Maybe he killed one of Cardo's friends. Maybe he stole Cardo's girl. I don't know what Deon's in for, and I don't feel right about asking.

"And how come he writing about how blacks be kept out of computers but not Latinos? You see a Hispanic Bill Gates around? You see any Guillermo Gates?"

There are actually three Hispanics in the computer class: Memmo, a kid named Inzy, and some super-quiet girl named Maria.

"That's an awesome question, Cardo. Why don't you write an article about that?"

"Naw," Cardo says. "But I get you a rap from Felipe knock your socks off."

"Great. I'll ask Deon to put it in the next newsletter."

"I got your word?"

"Well, yeah. We're trying to improve it. That's why we got Barbie Santiago to do an advice column."

"You got to be hard up you asking that Dominicana for advice."

"She's not that bad."

"Oh really? Like you and her are tight now?"

"I'm just saying she's not as bad as you said. There's more to her, that's all."

Cardo laughs that chimpy laugh of his. "Aw man, you so p-whipped right now. You don't even know it. You all, yeah, there's more to this bitch than a stone-cold killer. She care about me. Ooh." He hugs himself. "Let me tell you some-thing about Barbie Santiago, bro. That bitch a she-devil. Just ask Enrique Cabron. Dude was her *boyfriend*."

This is a detail I didn't know. We haven't gotten to Barbie's crime story in group yet. I figured Enrique Cabron was some banger who got on the wrong side of Sol D.

"Yeah," Cardo says. "Dude got into it with some other girl. Barbie's friend or something. Girl cried rape or some shit. So Barbie smoked him."

"Sounds like she did the world a favor."

"Yeah, except that friend of hers? The little puta with the tears running down her face, she moves straight on to Cabron's brother. Hell, the whole family having a piece of her."

"That girl, Barbie's friend, she have a name?"

"Yeah, she got a name. Mariana something. Why?"

The girl from Barbie's quinceañera story.

"Anyway," Cardo says. "Everybody knew that girl was com-munity property. Everyone 'cept Barbie Santiago. Bitch wants you to think she some avenging angel. Naw, man. She just a bitch with a vendetta."

"Right."

"What, you don't believe me? Suit yourself, bro, but keep your eyes open. That's all I'm saying. She be all patting you on the back like she your best friend, but watch out, ese, 'coz she got a knife in her hand."

Oh, that's another thing. *Everybody* has a knife in hand. The blacks, the whites, the guards, the cops, his lawyer, his counselor, even the mother of his unborn child who went from being "the light of my life" to a ho-bag he doesn't trust anymore. You'd think a fellow Latina like Barbie would get some kind of free pass, but no way. She's in the wrong gang.

In Cardo's mind, there's a shadow world under the surface of the regular world. But he's the only one who can see it. Everyone else is "living in a dream." The group therapy team he used to love? They're all suckers now. The life he dreamed about in Miami? That was a scam. And the more he rages about this shadow world, with its racism and unfairness, the closer it brings him to the Disciples. They're the only pure ones. They're the ones who have his back. He practically tears up when he talks about them.

"Well, you'll get a chance to see what Barbie's made of in the next newsletter," I tell him.

"I ain't reading that shit."

"Might be entertaining at least."

"I'll tell you what's entertaining. You print a rap by the Disciples instead of that pussy-ass no-rhyming bullshit by Javier Muñoz."

"Bring me one then. And it wasn't a rap, Cardo. It was a *poem.*"

CHAPTER 26

"Yo, we got problems."

Deon. In the computer room.

"I got guys coming up to me all day, handing me shit like this." He shoves a piece of paper in my face.

It's a poem called "The Face in the Dark." Apparently, this face appears whenever the poet, one Darius Johnstone, closes his eyes. The face is either a warning of evil things to come or a promise from his dead mother that angels are waiting for him in heaven. Johnstone doesn't seem to be sure which. When I finish reading that one, Deon hands me a stack of others. "I'm telling people you're in charge of this, since you started it," he says.

"In charge of what?"

"Poems and shit. Anyone got poems, essays, stories, or whatever, you take care of them."

"What am I supposed to do with them?"

"Pick out the ones you like. Type them up. Lay them out."

"Lay them out?"

"Yeah. You got to learn how to do that. Get me six different things. And mix it up. Some long, some short. Some funny. Some serious. Let's give the people what they want."

"I'm only here for another week, you know."

I shouldn't have said that. Having a short sentence at Haverland does not make you popular.

"All right, then you got one week to get me six things *and* find yourself a replacement. You started this. You gonna finish it."

"Smart move, Deon," Mr. Klein says. "Get kids to submit their own work, so now they're invested in reading it. Really smart."

"Yeah," Deon says. "And some people thought it'd be better if nobody read the damn thing. Ain't that right, Huang?"

"Whatever," Huang says. Then he rubs that great big ruby of a nose.

CHAPTER 27

Deon was right. Javier's poem was such a hit that now everyone wants in on the action. When word gets out that Isaac West is in charge of "poems and shit," that I'm the damn Poems and Shit Editor, they stop me everywhere—out in the yard, in the cafeteria, in the hallways. Sometimes they're all shy and embarrassed about it, shoving a crumpled-up napkin into my hand with some love note scrawled on it. Other times they march right up to me in full view of their friends and unfold a piece of paper like it's the Ten Commandments.

A lot of it is garbage: pissed off tirades about enemy gangs, lame personal beefs, or hopeless declarations of love for some girl who doesn't have the time of day. Someone even hands me a rhyming shopping list that includes "a gold-plated Hummer" (for "cruisin' in the summer") and "a hot tub full of big-ass bitches" (for "when you get those shaboink-boink itches"). Believe it or not, it gets worse.

Even Cecil Boone has something for me. He looks scared as a mouse walking up to me out in the yard. "Thanks, buddy," he says as he hands me this folded-up piece of paper that's so sweaty it must have been sitting in his bear-sized palm all morning. I can't be sure Boone remembers me from our "incident" in the cafeteria. But as he heads off on his trunk-sized legs, all I can think of is, *Yeah, man, thanks for not killing me.*

My career as Poems and Shit Editor will be short. But I figure I may as well throw myself into it. Turns out I *like* reading other people's stories, even the stupid ones. No, *especially* the stupid ones. People unload all kinds of crazy shit onto paper, things they'd never say out loud. Give me a textbook to read and it'll be a struggle just to get me to open the stupid thing. But scrawl some crazy-ass love poem onto a napkin, and you got me.

My favorite one is a poem by Tiana Grasley called "My Secret."

> *You came into my bedroom*
> *in the middle of the night.*
> *I never opened my eyes.*
> *I was pretending to sleep.*
> *Don't worry because I'll never tell.*
> *You can take my body*
> *but my words belong to me.*

I know some of the guys at Haverland are guilty of the secret Tiana's talking about. Sometimes I hear them bragging about their "hos" and "bitches" and it makes me want to kill every single one of them. Tiana's secret is as common as dirt. But there on the page it's something else. A battle cry. I can't wait to unleash it. I have six pieces to fill up the next issue of *The Free.* And they are going to explode people's heads.

That will be my parting gift to Haverland.

And in the meantime, before I clear out of here, I get a little bit of cred. You want your shit published, you've got to come to me, Isaac West. Normally, I've got no interest in being the man in charge of anything. I prefer to be invisible. But this little kingdom of poems and shit is just the right size for me, big enough to buy me some cred, small enough to keep that target off my back.

CHAPTER 28

Janelle is holding steady at Mrs. Rodriguez's house while Mom sucks up the luxury of rehab. If it turns out like all the other times, she'll stay sober just long enough for DCF to lose interest in her case. She knows that drill cold. Then she'll spend a few days actually believing she's turned a corner this time. She'll make vague promises about getting her GED or looking for a job somewhere in "accounts." Karen West does have bursts of promise from time to time. She knows how to act responsible. It's all bullshit, but it means Janelle and I will get a little break from the usual insanity at home, and I, for one, am looking forward to some peace.

There is no peace in the orange-rug room, though. It's Friday, my last day of group, and Dr. Horton is determined to make the most of it.

"I wish we had a little more time with you," he says. "I feel like we're just getting to know you, Isaac."

I like Dr. Horton. I don't meet too many people like him. He's the kind of guy you're supposed to think of as a role model. Not that I'm an expert in role models. Other than the dirtbags who buzz around my mother, I don't meet too many grown men at all. The only stable man in my life is Tom Flannery, but even I know you're not supposed to have a car thief as a role model. You take what you can get, though.

"So, how about one last role-play?" Dr. Horton says.

I'd prefer to spend my last day listening. We haven't gotten back to Sandra and her disappearing problem yet. And I still haven't heard Barbie's crime story. I'd like to connect the dots between that girl, Mariana, and Barbie's victim, Enrique Cabron. Listening is my favorite part of group and the thing I'm actually going to miss when I get out of here.

"What do you say?" Dr. Horton's making that "Here, have a cookie" face again. So obvious. "I want to leave you with something to work on when you get home. Something I think I've identified in your stories. A common thread, if you will. Humor me?"

"Yeah, come on, Ike," Barbie says.

Ike? When did I become *Ike* to her? Nobody calls me Ike.

"Don't you want your farewell gift?" she asks. "From all of us?"

"Yeah, something to remember us by," Wayne adds.

They won't let up. They love to throw themselves into character, get straight down into the rot with you. The uglier the better. I figure I owe them one more tumble to make up for that lie I told first time around. What a mistake that was. These people are way too sharp for a story like that.

"Sure," I say. "Why not."

"That a boy," Dr. Horton says. He passes out a script to Sandra, Barbie, Riley, and Wayne. "I want you to observe first time around," he tells me. "Why don't you wait outside with Javier while we block it."

Javier and I go out into the hall and sit with our backs against the cement wall. Javier looks tired.

"How long you been here?" I ask him.

"Eleven months. Still waiting for my court date."

"It can take that long?"

"Take as long as they want. What do I have to go back to?"

He stares at the radiator across the hallway, where clumps of gray fuzz have collected in the pipes. Every few seconds it burps out a hiss. "I did real good on all my role-plays though. I played my victim. I played myself. I even played that lady judge who sentenced me. I got straight up in her head too, felt the pain she had when she put me in here. She wasn't out to get me. Her hands just tied and she got hundreds of cases to get through. She just looking out for the community, that's all. I was right there." He presses his finger into his forehead.

I wonder if he wants me to say something, but I stay quiet.

"I didn't hide nothing," he goes on. "Man, that was rough. 'Coz I thought I'd already dealt with what I done, but no way. Not till you're reliving it. That's when you realize what you done. I was kind of like you. I didn't put the knife in Jorge Losado. But I didn't stop it, neither. Christ, I held him down while my brother did it. I didn't even realize how heavy that was until I got in *there*." He taps his knuckles on the door. "That's when it got mad real."

"Yeah?"

"Shit, yeah. I mean, on the night in question, I didn't even know what the hell I was doing. I was stoned out of my mind. But in there. I don't know. Maybe it's 'coz you don't have that adrenaline no more clogging up your brain, so you can *think*. Maybe it's 'coz you already know how it turns out, so there's no suspense or something. All's I know is something happens in there. Something real. If you let it. I mean, if you're honest."

I look at him.

"All I'm saying is you ain't the only one running away from shit in here," he says. "We all playing that game. And we got damn good reasons to run too. You think Sandra likes living with what she did? Or Riley?"

"What did Riley do?"

"He burned his best friend's house down. Snuck in with a can of gasoline while they were sleeping and lit the place up. Kid's mother got third-degree burns."

"Jesus. Why'd he do it?"

"Because the kid called him a pussy on Facebook or some shit. You know how that goes. But I'll tell you something. Riley gets in there and he tells it all. He doesn't hide nothing. We doing a role-play? Don't matter if it's his or someone else's. He's up in it. He's all the way there. Not just his mind, either. And this scene we're doing for you now? Come on, this is your last chance. There ain't no role-plays out in the free. So if it makes you feel something, go ahead and feel it. You know we ain't gonna ride you for it. You got tears, let 'em out. You should have seen Wayne when we did that role-play about how his dad beating on his mom. Dude was curled up on the floor, crying like a baby. And that wasn't just for Wayne's sake, neither. That was for all of us. 'Coz we all got some kind of pain like that in us. Ain't nobody winds up in juvie without there's some tears in his past."

The door cracks open and Riley pokes his head through. "We're ready for you."

CHAPTER 29

I sit next to Javier. In front of us are three chairs pressed together in a line. The cardboard box is emptied out and turned upside down on the floor in front of them. Barbie steps forward and motions for Riley to join her. Then she tells Sandra and Wayne to sit on the chairs. They refuse. Barbie stamps her foot and jabs her finger toward the chairs, but they stay put. Pissed off now, Barbie stalks over, grabs them both by the wrists and drags them to the chairs. They go limp and drop into the chairs, then stare straight ahead like they've given up.

I'm totally confused. Which one is Pat Healy? Which one is me? And who is Barbie playing?

It's only when Barbie takes *Riley's* hand and leads him to the door that I figure out which scene they're playing.

Javier nudges me with his knee. "Open your eyes," he whispers.

I don't even realize I've closed them.

When Barbie and Riley get to the door, Wayne rises from his seat to stop them, but Sandra grabs his hand and pulls him back down.

"Stay with me," she says.

Barbie glares at Wayne, then leaves the room with Riley. Eventually, Sandra tugs Wayne around so they can both stare at the cardboard box. It's supposed to be a television. The real television never worked, but my stupid mother kept dragging it from apartment to apartment, promising to fix it someday when she had the money.

It's that one-bedroom in Ashland. They're making me relive the worst day of my life. Are they punishing me for lying about my crime story? I thought I made up for that. I thought we were cool now. I ripped that page out of my notebook and tore it up.

For a whole minute nothing happens, just Wayne and Sandra sitting on those chairs. I watch the time pass on the clock. Then something thumps in the hallway. Wayne and Sandra whip around and face the door. Barbie cries out and Wayne rises to kneel on the chair, but Sandra pulls him back down.

Now something pounds against the door. Not a fist, something bigger, like someone's whole back. Barbie cries out again. Wayne stands up this time, but Sandra clings to his arm.

"Stay with me," she says.

Another thump, like Barbie's whole body getting slammed into the door. Wayne jerks toward it, but Sandra clings to him. He drops to his knees and rests his chin on the back of the chair. Sandra does the same thing and the two of them stare at the door without moving for a long time.

Out in the hallway, Barbie groans in pain. The second hand sweeps the clock six times. Barbie's cries get louder until something smothers them—a hand, a pillow, one of the foam bats? I can't tell. The door shakes. Something clatters to the floor.

The second hand keeps circling. It'll do that eight more times. Fourteen minutes. That's what I wrote in my notebook. That day in Ashland, I timed it with the clock on the broken DVD player. My mother never set it right, so it was always around five hours off. I never knew what time it was except when I was at school.

All I have to do now is wait it out while Barbie and Riley grunt and slap their thighs in the hallway. It's just a role-play. It isn't real. I'm not back in the living room of that one-bedroom shelter in Ashland. There's no smell of piss and garbage seeping through the front door. I'm not sweating because we have no AC. I'm not listening to my mother and some scumbag in another room, hoping someone will call the cops about the noise. I'm not shoulder to shoulder with Janelle on that couch, praying to a God I don't believe in to wake me up from a nightmare I know is no nightmare. Eight more minutes and this will all be over.

"Open your eyes," Javier whispers.

But they *are* open. I'm sure of it. Only I'm not in the orange-rug room anymore. My body has left. It's drifting up through the white ceiling tiles. I'm in another room now, on another floor. Barbie's cries get small, like a voice on a radio in a passing car. Wayne and Sandra shrink into dots.

"Ike, what are you doing?"

Who is that? I don't recognize his voice.

"Isaac, you need to sit down."

I don't recognize that voice, either. I don't know any of these people. Maybe I used to. They're so far away. I can barely hear them because there's a louder voice inside my head saying, *"Stoppleasestoppleasestoppleasestop."*

"Dr. Horton, should we . . ."

My two legs walk toward a guy and a girl kneeling backward on some chairs. The girl's name is Sandra. The guy's name is Wayne. They're pretending to be other people. They're actors in a play. My hand reaches for Sandra's hand. She looks scared, confused, but she takes it. My hand makes

Sandra stand up. My body leads her to the door. I have to tug her along because she doesn't want to come. My hand opens the door and pushes Sandra through.

Outside in the hallway is a beautiful girl whose name is Barbie Santiago. She has orange-blond hair and black roots. Standing next to her is a chubby white kid named Riley. I *know* these people, but in this moment I can't remember how. They look worried and confused. But my body knows what to do. My hand takes Barbie's and pulls her into the orange-rug room, leaving Sandra to take her place in the hallway next to Riley. Sandra shakes her head, but my hand closes the door on her and that is that. I lead Barbie toward the couch, which is really just three chairs pressed together. I make her sit down next to Wayne.

Behind me, Javier whispers, "Oh God."

Someone must have punched Wayne or kicked him when I wasn't looking, because he looks like he's in pain now. He says, "You mean it was your sister?"

It's a question but I don't answer it, because I'm not really there. I'm in another room, on another floor. I'm not even watching from above anymore. I'm flying away.

"What should we do?" Wayne asks.

"Go with it," Dr. Horton says.

"This shit's too heavy," Wayne says.

Barbie takes Wayne's hand. "Shh," she says. "Mama's got you."

Wayne's eyes bulge, but he gives in to her. He faces front and stares at that TV, which in some reality is just an empty box on the floor.

Something thumps against the door. Wayne tears his hand from Barbie's and stands up. But Barbie, who is in no mood to take any crap from him, pulls him right back down. Another thump and Wayne's head whips around to the door.

Barbie grabs his chin with her free hand and forces him to face front.

"Stay with me," she says again.

Wayne shakes his head free. He wants to stand up and leave. His feet are pointing toward the door like he's ready to sprint for it. But something has him hypnotized.

Out in the hall Sandra cries.

Keep crying, I think. *Keep crying so I can find you and we can disappear together.*

Now Wayne is crying too. He tries to stuff it down. His cheeks puff out. He keeps trying to tug his hand out of Barbie's, but Barbie won't let go. And even though she's smaller than he is, for some reason she seems bigger. Wayne can't move. His shoulders shake and his brown skin shines with tears and snot.

Get up, Wayne, I think. *You could punch Barbie Santiago and go through that door. You could make all the crying stop, which is what you're supposed to be doing. Why don't you do that, Wayne? Why don't you punch Barbie Santiago's lights out right now? Why are you obeying her? Why aren't you saving Janelle?*

CHAPTER 30

I have no memory of leaving the orange-rug room. I don't remember dragging that old leather chair from some office and standing on it to shake the bars free from a window. I don't remember anything. So Ms. Jomolca has to tell me all of this from the edge of my mattress on the padded floor of a windowless cell.

I'm in solitary. That much, I figure out on my own.

"You don't remember kicking Dr. Horton?" Ms. Jomolca asks. There's no echo in the room. Her voice sounds close, flat.

"Or jumping off that chair and body-slamming Wayne Dugal?"

"Dugal?"

"He's a member of your team. You do remember your teammates, right?"

Their names come swimming up to me, but blended together like WaySanRivierSantiago.

"Am I asleep?" I hear my voice say. It sounds like someone else. "Is this a dream?"

Ms. Jomolca sighs. "They told me the drugs should have worn off by now. Why don't you get some rest, Isaac. I'll come back."

A dream then. I'm still asleep. I lie back on the mattress and close my eyes.

CHAPTER 31

It's a guard with my breakfast tray who gets me to understand how I wound up in solitary. A meaty white guy with no hair at all. He tells me I've been "totally out of it" for two days, after having something called a "psycho break." There's a plate of scrambled eggs on the tray that look real, not from powder. There's toast too, with butter spread all the way to the crust rather than just smeared in a thin stripe. There are two little packets of grape jelly.

"Perk of solitary," the guard tells me. "You get staff food. But don't get used to it." He puts the tray down on the padded floor right next to the mattress.

When I sit up, the room spins for a few seconds. "What's a psycho break?" My voice is hoarse.

"I don't know the *technical* definition," the guard says. "But basically you went ape shit. My associates had to tranq you up. You been here for two days, sleeping mostly, talking to yourself. You're gonna behave nice now, right?"

I blink at him. "Talking to myself?"

"The drugs'll make you do that."

"What did I say?"

"Same shit they all say. *Urgh oohmph blegh.*"

"Did I hurt anyone?"

"You kicked Dr. Horton in the chin."

I try to dig up the memory but it's not there. "How could I do that?"

"You're asking me?"

"No, I mean Dr. Horton is six foot four. How could I kick that high?"

"You were standing on a chair. You were trying to escape."

Now it comes to me, not all the details, but the need to escape: the feeling of flying away, straight through the prison walls, like they were made of air.

"You tried to bust through a barred window," the guard says. "Which, incidentally, would have dropped you straight into the yard. Which is fenced in *and* under constant surveillance."

"I wasn't trying to bust out."

The guard heads to the door. "Of course not. Eat something. It's been two days." He unlocks the door and disappears.

A click of the lock, then it's quiet again, a quiet that's thick and soft. But not comforting, not thick and soft like a blanket or a big couch. It's more like quicksand, something that wants you dead or at least buried alive.

I try to jump-start my brain but it won't tick over. I look at the tray with its plastic-wrapped spoon and little packets of salt and pepper. The eggs are still warm. I scoop them up and they're more delicious than my brain can handle. I don't think I've ever had food this good. I start stuffing them down, filling up a big hole of hunger that opened up out of nowhere. I drain the orange juice in one gulp. It's real, not powdered, with actual bits of pulp in it. This is the single best meal I have ever eaten. I start to tear up a little bit. That's how good it is.

Then something clicks. The memories come back.

I kicked Dr. Horton. I body-slammed Wayne. I tried to force myself through a barred window.

I let a stranger rape Janelle.

With the smell of grape jelly still hanging in the air, I puke the whole meal onto the padded beige floor.

CHAPTER 32

"You were thirteen," Ms. Jomolca says.

We're in her office now. I've been released from solitary, and the drugs are wearing off.

"She was ten," I tell her. My voice is rusty again because I haven't spoken since talking to the guard.

The door to her office is closed, which makes it feel even smaller than usual.

"What happened in that room sounds to me like a breakthrough," she says.

"Aren't I supposed to be in court today?"

"I was going to ask for an extension."

"No." My body tenses. I'm awake now.

"Just for a few weeks. I think you could really use the time to—"

"*No.* Please don't."

"Isaac, this is a major development. We can't just leave it unexamined."

"Yes, we can."

"It was your team who helped you get here. They want to help you through it."

"No."

"Isaac."

"I said no. I want to go to court. It's been thirty days. That was the deal."

"All I'm talking about is two weeks, Isaac, maybe three. I think you could really use the time to talk about this."

"I don't want to talk about it."

"But it could help you."

"It's not about me!"

Ms. Jomolca's face hardens. She's not the kind of lady who lets kids raise their voices at her. But she must know how much I'm hurting, because she lets it go.

"I've been good," I plead. "I did what I was supposed to. I told the truth about Sal Christaldi. I told the truth about everything. I did my role-play. I let my team keep hammering me. I let them way up into my shit. I did everything you asked me to. Why do you want to punish me?"

"I don't want to punish you, Isaac. I want to help you."

"Then send me home. Please, Ms. Jomolca. Please just send me home."

CHAPTER 33

My dismissal hearing is held at Stafford County Juvenile Court, in the ugly room where I got that "defendant capped plea." The judge, the Honorable Dorset Hayes, is in the same shitty mood I left him in thirty days ago.

Mine isn't any better. The memories have been coming hard and fast ever since I left Ms. Jomolca's office. The way Janelle called out for our mother, then for me. The way our mother rushed in to her afterward. How she closed the door so I couldn't see. Their quiet voices while Janelle cried and our mother tried to comfort her. The look on that man's face when he left the apartment, like he knew it was wrong but he wasn't about to stick around and apologize for it. These memories are sharp now, bold and bright, like they've been biding their time, waiting for their moment to come out of hiding. They're out and they're going to shine, damn it. Take up some space, see how much damage they can do.

Ms. Jomolca spends about half an hour up at the bench, walking the judge through some papers. I have no idea what she's written, whether she got to use all those words she likes so much, whether she's about to make Judge Hayes feel wise enough to send me home.

My lawyer sits next to me, thumbing his phone under the table. He hasn't said a word. He's probably still pissed at me for refusing to give up Pat Healy. He probably thinks I'm a waste of his time. The feeling is mutual. I'm looking forward to never having to see that pale head and that stupid dog-shaped ketchup stain again.

When Ms. Jomolca comes back to our table, I sit up a little straighter. I want to make Judge Hayes think I'm "transformed." But Judge Hayes isn't even looking at me. He's scowling at some papers Ms. Jomolca left behind.

"I don't understand what you're trying to tell me here, Ms. Jomolca. I'm reading this incident report, and I'm not seeing a violence-free term at Haverland."

"That's true, Your Honor," she says. "But the incident in question occurred during a group therapy session." Ms. Jomolca seems different here, timid, eager to please—not her usual fierce self. "Dr. Horton and I don't believe Isaac was actually trying to hurt anyone."

Judge Hayes lifts a piece of paper off his desk and reads from it. "The subject kicked Dr. Neil Horton in the chin, then leapt off the chair onto another minor and knocked him to the floor." He looks up from the paper with a scowl. "And this was after trying to *escape?*"

"Your Honor, Dr. Horton and I believe the defendant was in the grip of a dissociative episode."

The judge purses his lips like he's just bitten into some rotten candy. Then he rereads the report.

I haven't said a word so far. I'm hoping to make it through the whole hearing without opening my mouth. I can't defend my behavior that day, so why try? I can hardly remember it. The tranquilizers have fogged it up, made it seem like a dream rather than something that actually happened. It's only the guilty feeling in my stomach that tells me I really did those things.

"Miss Jomolca, whether he was trying to escape or having

some kind of . . . dissociative episode, are you going to tell me that this young offender is not violent?"

Ms. Jomolca's chest rises and falls underneath her navy blue blazer. "Your Honor, as stated, Dr. Horton and I both believe that the dissociative episode was the result of—"

"Are you talking about a repressed memory?"

"No. No, I'm not. I don't believe the science on repressed memories is very good, Your Honor."

"Good. Because I'm not interested in going down that road."

"If I could just explain, Your Honor . . . What some people refer to as repressed memories are actually, I believe, the result of a blending of true and false narratives around a traumatic event. In this case, Isaac's witnessing the rape of his sister."

The judge leans back, takes a deep breath, then narrows his eyes at me. "Go on," he says.

"He felt guilty," Ms. Jomolca says. "Responsible in some way, so he altered the memory into something more palatable, something he could live with, namely the rape of his mother instead. His mother was a prostitute and had frequent . . . visitors in the apartment. At any rate, because of the efforts of Dr. Horton and the other members of Isaac's therapy group to break down Isaac's defenses, that false or blended memory became unstable. As the true memory surfaced, he panicked and dissociated. Believe it or not, this is a good sign. It demonstrates Isaac's openness to the therapeutic process. He let those kids in, Your Honor. He revealed something to them that he'd hidden from everyone, even from himself."

The judge starts nodding, and Ms. Jomolca takes it as a sign to continue.

"It's not the first time we've seen this kind of behavior,

Your Honor. The group therapy process, especially the role-plays, often results in extreme eruptions of emotion. We think that's why it works so well. It helps to break down their defenses, open them up to a renewed sense of empathy."

There it is. One of her favorite words.

The judge nods. He likes that word too.

"Did you read the letter from Dr. Horton?" she asks. "He takes full responsibility for the incident. He believes he may have let the role-play go too far. That Isaac might not have been ready for it just yet."

"I read the letter. And I understand no one at Haverland is recommending disciplinary action?"

"No, they're not."

"And the other boy is unharmed?"

"Yes, Your Honor. He's fine."

I haven't seen Wayne or any of my teammates since that day. All going well, I'll never have to see them again.

"Sounds like you're doing some good work over there," Judge Hayes says. "Giving these kids a chance to work out some difficult issues in a safe environment."

Ms. Jomolca nods eagerly. "That's our mission."

"We need more of that kind of thing in juvenile justice," he goes on. "Instead of this hunger people have for locking kids up. As if that's going to solve anything."

I sneak a look at my lawyer to get his reaction to this, but he's a blank. Either he doesn't know where the judge is going with this or he doesn't care.

"Well I'm happy to say I agree with you, Ms. Jomolca," the judge says. "Sounds to me like young Isaac here has had some kind of a breakthrough, whatever you want to call it. I hope he understands how lucky he is that people like you and Dr. Horton show up every day to do this difficult work."

Judge Hayes looks directly at me now.

I put on my best "transformed" face. You're not supposed to talk unless the judge asks you to. But I am sucking up big-time, only with my body language. If my body could talk, it would be saying: *Yes, Your Honor. I know how lucky I am. I am the luckiest kid in the world. And totally transformed too. With a renewed sense of empathy. Oh my God, I have so much empathy right now. Thank you, Your Honor. Thank you so much for being so wise. It's an honor to receive your unbelievable wisdom.*

"Which is why I'm sending him back to Haverland," he says.

All the air flies out of my lungs, then from the room, then from the world.

"I can see no reason to send him home," he continues. "I understand there's a great deal of instability there? A run-away sister? A mother with a substance-abuse problem?" He starts flipping through my file.

Ms. Jomolca breaths once, deeply. "Yes, Your Honor."

"It's a good thing we have a spot for him at Haverland, then. Isaac, stand up."

I look at my lawyer, who waves for me to get up. I'm shaking but I manage to push my chair back with an awful screech.

"Based on your behavior while incarcerated, the details of your crime, and the situation at home, I'm sending you back to Haverland for one more year."

My mouth flies open. I have to grip the edge of the table to keep standing. My lawyer puts a hand on my shoulder.

"Don't think of this as punishment," Judge Hayes says. "Think of it as an opportunity. Haverland's different. That's why I sent you there in the first place. You can get your diploma there, pick up some extra computer training, which apparently you're already doing. You've got Dr. Horton and Ms. Jomolca there. This is all good, Isaac. Look at me."

Judge Hayes's face is stern, no-nonsense. He believes he's

doing me a favor by sending me back to Haverland. What about Janelle? She's not just some "runaway." It makes me sick to hear him describe her like that, like she's part of my problem. She's not. She's my saving grace. She's the one beautiful thing in my rotten life. Can't he understand why Janelle would run away? Was he even listening to what Ms. Jomolca told him about our mother, about Ashland?

In a panic I turn to my lawyer. "Pat Healy," I say. "The giant's name is Patrick Healy. He's the one who beat up Sal Christaldi. It wasn't me. I was only covering for him—"

"Counselor," the judge spits out. "What is your client babbling about?"

Slater finally opens his mouth, and he doesn't seem happy about it. "I'm sorry, Your Honor. Can I please have a moment with him?"

"What kind of courtroom do you think I'm running here? I'm ordering him back to Haverland so he can learn to control himself."

"But it wasn't me, Your Honor." My voice rises as I glance between the judge and my lawyer. "It was Healy who hit Mr. Christaldi. I only took the rap to keep him out of jail. Tell him, Mr. Slater. Tell him about how Mr. Christaldi said it was a giant who hit him. A white kid. That's not me. It can't be. It was Patrick Healy—"

"Shh," Slater hisses.

The judge brings his gavel down three times. That's the end of the hearing.

CHAPTER 34

That night, I'm treated to another stay in solitary. I don't get the drugs though. I'm supposed to spend the time "coming to terms" with the judge's decision. I don't come to terms with anything. Instead I spend the night pacing the tiny room while wondering how long it's going to take for that ADA lady to track down Pat Healy and cut me a deal.

It's a filthy piece of business selling him out like that, but it's not like I had a choice. I can't stick around juvie for another year. Not with Janelle at home. Mom all broken inside and out. She can't earn a living her usual way. What's that going to lead to?

I did what I had to do. If Healy doesn't get that, he's a fool. He *is* a fool, already, going nuts on Mr. Christaldi like that. What did he think was going to happen? It serves him right, getting busted for it. He's lucky I ever agreed to take the rap for him in the first place. And even luckier that Mr. Flannery doesn't kick him out of his crew.

I get an even sicker feeling when I think about Mr. Flannery. I wonder if there's any chance he'll see things my way on this. Sure, loyalty to your crew is important, but a sister is a sister. That's blood. What kind of a brother would I be if I left Janelle hanging like that, at my mother's mercy? Mr. Flannery has to understand that. He'd be a monster not to.

CHAPTER 35

The next morning, a guard brings me from solitary straight to Ms. Jomolca's office. I haven't slept at all.

"I'm totally jammed today," she says. "But I wanted to see how you're holding up."

"I'm okay. Is Mr. Slater coming?"

"Did you have an appointment?"

"No. I just thought, I don't know, maybe I'd have to make an official statement or something, or a deposition or whatever, about Pat Healy? Have they arrested him?"

"Actually, I got an email from your lawyer early this morning . . ." She digs her phone out of the pocket of her coat and scrolls through her messages. "They're having trouble finding Patrick Healy. His mother says he never came home last night. Does he have a girlfriend or anything? Anyplace where he might be staying?"

I don't know about any girlfriends. As for where Healy could be staying, it could be anywhere. If he knows the cops are after him, maybe he skipped town. Maybe Mr. Flannery is hiding him somewhere.

"No," I say. "I don't know where he could be."

"You didn't contact him, did you? After your hearing?"

"No."

"Strange."

"What do you mean?"

"Well, according to your lawyer, his mother said he rarely stays out late. And that he's never not come home."

Word must have gotten to him somehow.

"You're sure you didn't call him? Or call someone else who could have told him?"

"I haven't called anyone. I came right back here from court and straight into solitary, remember? If Healy knows I gave him up, it's not from me. This isn't going to change things, is it?"

"What things?"

"My plea deal? If they can't find him, does that mean I don't get the deal?"

"What deal?"

"For giving up Healy."

"Who said you're getting a deal for giving up Healy? Isaac, the judge's ruling has nothing to do with Patrick Healy. He sent you back here because of what happened with Dr. Horton."

"But even Dr. Horton said that was his fault. You wrote that in your report. Didn't you?"

"Well, yes, Isaac, I did. But the judge wasn't persuaded. You were there. You heard him. He wants you back here."

"But that's not fair. Can't that ADA lady talk to him? Tell him how I helped her? It's not *my* fault they can't find Healy. I still gave him up."

"Isaac, did your lawyer lead you to believe that identifying Patrick Healy would nullify the judge's ruling? Did he actually say that to you?"

"Well, no, but—"

"What did he say?" She's staring at me now, hard.

"Just that he was going to talk to the ADA and see what she could do for me."

"Well, yes, Isaac, what she can do for you is drop that perjury charge. You have to understand, the judge's ruling is final. It's not like in the movies, where you sell someone out and walk free. This is *juvenile* justice. You're here because your life is basically in Judge Hayes's hands. That's the flip side of that short sentence you got. I admit I was surprised by his ruling. I actually disagreed with it, at first. But I think we need to look on the bright side."

I shake my head furiously, refusing to accept what she's saying. "I can't stay here."

"I know you want to go home, but think about what you'd be going home to."

"I *have* to go home."

She shakes her head. "You're not looking at this the right way, Isaac. You're not seeing all that you have here: I don't know if you realize this, Isaac, but Haverland is not like most juvenile detention centers. Most of them are just a warm-up for jail, with about as much opportunity for rehabilitation. But here you have friends, responsible adults who care about you, who have time for you. And I heard about that newsletter too. I think it's great that you're—"

"So I'm not getting out? Oh my God, you're telling me I gave up Healy for *nothing?*"

CHAPTER 36

It's the usual crowd of mothers and girlfriends in the visitors' room on Wednesday. A few kids run around making a nuisance of themselves. Their mother, some skinhead's white trash girlfriend, yells at them. All the women in here are pissed off about something, always. This is what I've got to look forward to for another year.

"I don't understand," Janelle says. "I thought it was supposed to be thirty days. That's what you said."

"It was."

"So what happened?"

"I fucked up, Janelle. I fucked up real bad." I don't dare tell her exactly *how*, of course. My final role-play, my freakout, my "dissociative episode." That all leads back to Ashland, and we don't talk about Ashland.

"So when *are* you getting out?"

"A year."

Her breath catches, just like mine did when Judge Hayes dropped the news. She looks suspicious for a second, like she's waiting for me to tell her it's all a sick joke and I'm getting out today. Ha-ha, gotcha!

"We've got to be smart now," I tell her. "We've got to plan."

She knows that punchline isn't coming now. She showed up today because she wanted to know why I wasn't home yet. She figured it was some legal technicality, some paper-work our mother forgot to sign. She wasn't expecting bad news this big, and when it finally hits her, she collapses on me. She's so small inside that puffy coat. Her thin back and skinny shoulders feel so fragile.

I hold her while she cries. There's nothing I can say. There's no silver lining to any of this. There's no angle that makes this any better than what it is.

"Listen to me, Janelle." I grip her by the shoulders and sit her up. I can't get emotional now. We have to plan. Janelle knows the drill. She knows exactly how much room there is in her life to feel sorry for herself. About one minute. Then she has to suck it up and get down to the nuts and bolts. And that minute is up. She wipes her face clean, sniffs back the rest of her tears.

"Take the money from the doll under your bed," I tell her.

"No. We're saving that. That's our first month's rent."

"Take it. Don't let Mom know it's there. Take it and pay the rent. Go to Mrs. Pretzinger's apartment upstairs and pay it in cash. Get a receipt too. Then buy some food. Buy stuff that lasts. Rice, canned things, you know. Tell Mom it's from the church or something. Do *not* let her know you have money."

"I can't do this."

"Yes, you can. There's twelve hundred dollars in there. That's a few months' rent, right?"

"I don't know. I don't know how much it costs."

"Look, we just have to keep things calm. She's sober now, right?"

Janelle nods.

"Maybe it'll last this time."

"Isaac."

"No, maybe it will. With me gone, she's gonna have to

work even harder to keep you. Now you got that guidance counselor in your corner. DCF on her case."

Janelle stares at me for a minute, then she laughs gently. "Yeah, sure," she says. "Maybe it'll last this time." She's already working through the possibilities. I can see it in her eyes. She's thinking ahead, seeing into the future. Our mother is sober now. When she comes out of rehab, she's always meek as a kitten. But it never lasts. Give it a few weeks and she'll twist herself right back into her usual self. That's when Janelle is going to run. She'll wait as long as she can, let our mother run down the clock on being sober. Then she'll make her escape. She's already mapping her route.

"Wherever you go, Janelle . . ." My voice fails me. "Take that money with you. All of it."

"That money is *ours*."

"No, Janelle, it's yours."

"But we—"

"It's not about me." I hold her small face in my hands. What I see in her eyes isn't myself anymore, my younger twin. I see the young woman she's becoming—scared, *scarred*, tough, but still just a kid. I love her so much I can't figure out how it's even possible that I failed her so badly, why the world didn't rise to the challenge and rescue her. Why doesn't it ever do that? Why doesn't it care?

CHAPTER 37

That night in our cell, Cardo makes the very wise choice of giving me a wide berth, or at least what passes for one in a ten-foot-by-six-foot cell. My eyes are red. I don't even bother hiding the fact that I've been crying all day. I don't care who knows. Cardo doesn't mention it at first. He has his own problems. And he has his body to keep himself busy. He's always doing push-ups and sit-ups these days, huffing and puffing his way through them, admiring himself in that dirty mirror.

He can't live with silence for long, though. If his mouth isn't moving, he gets nervous.

"What the fuck happen to you anyway?" he says. "A few days to go and you pull that shit? Fucking stupid, man."

I just look at him. I have nothing left for Cardo. I can't even get mad at him.

"Guys saying you hit a guard or something. That true?"

When I don't answer, Cardo gets the picture and goes back to his mirror. He runs a finger down some new vein in his shoulder. "Well, you only got yourself to blame being in here now, homes. How's that feel?"

For a second I picture myself grabbing Cardo by the head and smashing his monkey face into that mirror. I picture the blood and the spit. I see Cardo's ropy arms trying to punch me away, my hands slipping around his neck. I can feel myself contracting into a hard nut of rage. It's the same feeling I had before I punched Sean McKenzie.

Before it gets the better of me I slide down the wall and rest my chin on my knees. *Could* I kill someone? Me? Isaac West? The idea settles like a blanket around my shoulders. It's only the pain making me think this way. The guilt. The anger. But the idea won't disappear. It's not a blanket. It's my own shadow. It's part of me. Where I go, it goes. And it's more than an idea. It's a plan. Yes, I'm capable of it. Of course I am. Underneath those layers of rot and despair, my soul cries out in agony and rage and this is its prayer:

Kill. Kill and it will all end.

There's even a kind of logic to it. If you get down to the cold business of who actually deserves to die, you can make a case. You can make a damn good case.

"Your mother's a whore," I say.

"The fuck you just say?" Cardo peels himself from that mirror, ready to throw down. "You talkin' 'bout my mother?"

"Not *your* mother," I tell him. "Mine. That's what that kid said."

"What kid?"

"Sean McKenzie."

"The hell's he?"

"Some white kid at my old school."

"He called your mother a whore?"

"Yeah."

"So what'd you do?"

"I punched him."

"Good."

"I got expelled for it."

"That's bullshit. You don't be calling someone's mother a whore if you ain't asking to get beat."

"Principal didn't see it that way."

"Yeah, I bet. You some white kid, you'd a got a slap on the wrist."

"I had to transfer to Donverse Vocational. That's how I met my partner, started stealing cars."

"Aw, don't be playing that game."

"What game?"

Cardo turns back to the mirror and flexes his arms at his sides. "The backdoor game. If only I done that different, then this wouldn't have happened and that wouldn't have happened."

"Yeah, but it's true. If Sean McKenzie didn't call my mother a whore, I wouldn't be here right now."

"So everything's Sean McKenzie's fault? That what you're saying?"

"No." I collapse on my bed and stare up at the springs of Cardo's bunk. "It's my mother's fault."

"How's it your mother's fault?"

"Because my mother's a whore."

"The hell you talking about?"

"It's true. I'm not saying Sean McKenzie should have said it out loud like that, in front of his friends. But it happens to be true. My mother *is* a whore. And if she wasn't, none of this would have happened."

"If it weren't for her, you wouldn't be here."

"That's what I'm saying."

"No, Homes. If it weren't for your mother, you wouldn't *be here*. As in *alive*."

"Well, I guess that's her fault then too."

Cardo moves in on his mirror for a closer look. "You're not making any sense."

It may not make sense to Cardo. But it's all starting to make sense to Isaac West. My mother is the reason I punched Sean McKenzie, got expelled, and wound up at Donverse

Vocational. She's also the reason I had to steal cars in the first place. She's the reason Janelle is in danger at home and the reason I have to send her to boarding school. At the bottom of every shitty thing that's ever happened, going all the way back to the beginning of my life, there's Karen West.

"I wish she was dead."

Cardo turns from the mirror and wags his finger at me like some old lady. "You need to take that back, ese. I don't care what she does for a living. She still your mom. And a mother is *sacred*."

I chuckle. I don't doubt for a second that Cardo believes this line of bull. They all do. If you ever want to see a hard case cry, tell him a story about a kindhearted mother. It doesn't matter that his own mother tried to sell him for crack once. Mothers are saints. End of story. Javier's mother dumped him outside a hospital with a note pinned to his diaper when he was nine months old. He *still* loves her, blames himself for coming along at the wrong time.

I must be the only kid at Haverland who isn't under that voodoo spell. A mother isn't a saint in my book. A mother is just a woman who got herself knocked up. If you want to be a saint, you have to do better than that.

I close my eyes. That's when the idea starts to take shape. Before, it was just a dark feeling, a hunger. Now it's an actual possibility. I open my eyes again.

"You could make it happen, Cardo."

"Make what happen?"

"Oh come on, don't play dumb."

But Cardo isn't playing. He honestly has no idea what I'm talking about.

Until he does.

"Aw no," he says.

"It would solve everything."

"No way, man. You ain't thinking straight."

But I *am* thinking straight, straighter than I've ever thought before. If I want to protect Janelle from my mother, what better way to do it?

"You want to put a hit on your own mother?"

"Why not?"

"Because that's some evil shit. You don't come back from that."

Of course it's evil to Cardo; he's under the spell. I shut up and let him talk. He has plenty to say on the subject. The idea is diabolical, the devil's work. It's against nature, psychotic, and wronger than all the wrong things in the world combined, plus more wrong on top of that. But, after a while, I can see him coming around. He's working too hard to convince me. He's trying to convince himself. And you can't miss that flicker of excitement in his eyes.

Hell, it's *my* mother we're talking about. Not his.

This is an opportunity if you look at it the right way. And Cardo's looking all right. He's an ambitious little fucker, especially now that he's back with the Disciples. He doesn't want to be some bit player. He's "Jefe material." Always has been. My proposition may be outrageous, but it touches something in Cardo, something deep and hungry. And I know just how to work that particular angle.

"Come on, Cardo. You could be my miracle."

CHAPTER 38

It's a shitty plan. I know that. But life, as I'm sure you've guessed by now, is not a series of best-case scenarios. You play the cards you're dealt, which in my case is a two and a four, a joker, and a torn coupon for tampons with a nine and a heart drawn on it. But once my mother is gone, DCF will have to place Janelle somewhere. Anywhere is better than where she is now. Maybe Mrs. Rodriguez will take her in.

I sit dead-eyed through all of my classes, wondering how Cardo will pull it off. Will he actually do it? I'm not stopping him. I'm not calling the whole thing off. I don't feel guilty about it either. In fact, it's the first time in a long time I don't feel guilty. I know I probably will someday, once the hate has cooled down and the few happy memories I have of my mother have room to breathe. Like that time she gave Janelle and me twenty bucks and sent us to the carnival in the vacant lot around the corner. We spent it on the scariest, sickest rides, and when we ran out of money, we waited for her at the gate and she bought us both fried dough.

Sure, there were some good times. But that changes nothing. Karen West made this bed. Now she's about to lie in it.

Forever.

CHAPTER 31

"Ten thousand dollars," Cardo whispers when he gets back to our cell that night. "You ain't got that, we got problems."

"Ten thousand?" I whisper back. He may as well have said ten *billion*.

"Any chance you can get your mom down to Mexico? 'Coz I can get it done for, like, five hundred bucks in Mexico City. Shit, they'd probably do it for a Yankees cap down there."

I slump onto my bunk. "Yeah, Cardo. Now that she's out of rehab, I think she's planning on taking one of them cruises to Cancun."

Cardo snickers, then goes back to his mirror. I've never seen anyone so in love with himself. He's especially in love with his shoulders. "Sorry, man. Why don't you steal a few more of them Escalades, then we'll talk."

It's easy come, easy go for Cardo. His ambition can wait for the next opportunity to come around, which it definitely will. But for me, this is the end of the road. I've got twelve hundred dollars in that doll under Janelle's bed. But even if Janelle hasn't already spent it on rent and food, I'm good enough at math to know that ten thousand minus twelve hundred is more money than I can get my hands on.

CHAPTER 40

When you coming back to group?

That's Barbie emailing me from across the computer room. I sit as far away from her as possible now because I can't face her. I can't face any of them. Luckily I don't have to. I'm stuck at Haverland for another year no matter what I do. Group therapy is voluntary now. And I volunteer not to go anymore. Great incentive system, right? Way to be wise, Judge Hayes. I can feel the waves of rehabilitation washing over me. You're right. Haverland really is special.

I ignore Barbie's email, but this is not a reaction she's down with.

> *Dr. Horton's all broke up about it. He won't talk but I can tell. You gonna let him think he messed up your head? That's cold. Man only trying to do some good. Got a bunch of criminal psychopaths to deal with. Cut him some slack, Ike.*

I ignore this one too. I've got enough on my mind without having to worry about Dr. Horton's *feelings*. Dr. Horton's feelings go in a box labeled NOT ISAAC WEST'S PROBLEM. Barbie has a different take on this, though. She stalks over and stands behind the kid using the laptop next to me. He's new, some black kid who never says anything. He's working on Stanley Huang's All-Important, Life-Changing Word-Processing Tutorial, and he's as happy about that as I was. When he finally gets around to noticing Barbie hovering like the Grim Reaper, he turns practically white. Barbie points to the laptop she's just left on the other side of the room.

"Stanley," she says. "This young man's gonna need you to set him up over there, 'kay? Thanks, big guy."

Stanley does as he's told, the little pussy. Big guy, my ass. Stanley Huang weighs less than me. But Barbie knows how to stoke his ego. She takes the kid's seat and pulls it closer to me.

"You think you're the only one got something like that in your past?" she whispers.

"I'm not talking about it, Barbie."

"Fine."

She starts typing on the kid's laptop. A few seconds later I get an IM.

—*You don't cut out on your group. That's low.*

I know her well enough to know she's not going away. So I IM her back.

—*Why do you care if I come back or not? What difference it make to you?*

—*It's called loyalty, Ike. What are you blind deaf and dumb or something? You honestly telling me you didn't feel something in there soon as you told the truth? You got in deep with us. That's why the shit went down. Because you stopped lying to us.*

I laugh out loud.

"What's so funny?" she says.

"You are."

"Oh, is that it? You just gonna laugh it all off now, like it's nothing. Like *we're* nothing."

"I'm laughing because I never told you the truth. I told you the bare minimum. I told you what I could get away with."

"The hell you talking about?"

Just then, I notice a new email in my inbox. It's from Ian. Slater@publiccounsel.com. Now that it's too late to mean anything, I actually remember my lawyer's name. The first thing I notice in his email is the photograph of Pat Healy. His face is all puffy and his eyes are closed. He looks like hell, like maybe the cops did a number on him when they picked him up.

> *Hi Isaac. Can you just confirm for me that this is Patrick Healy, your accomplice? I know the photo's not great. The ADA would like your confirmation so she can close the case. I'm sorry to report he was found dead in Revere. Drug para-phernalia found at the scene indicate an overdose. It was near a well-known shooting gallery. Regards, Ian Slater.*

When I look up, Barbie's reading over my shoulder. She reaches across me and hits the up arrow so she can see the photograph herself.

"That your partner?"

I ignore her. I hit reply and type, "That's Healy."

Barbie stares at me, those amber eyes burning holes through my head. But I can't pull my eyes away from Healy's dead face. He doesn't look peaceful or angelic, the way people sometimes describe a dead person. He looks destroyed.

"Heroin," Barbie says. "He into that shit?"

"No."

"You sure?"

I shrug. I *thought* I was sure. Healy had to pee in that cup just like I did. Flannery wouldn't take him onto his crew unless he was clean, relative or not.

"Sorry, man," Barbie says. She taps my shoulder with her fist, then goes back to her laptop.

"You getting me those pieces or what?" Deon asks me. "'Coz if you ain't up to it, I got to replace you."

"Naw, I'm on it," I tell him. "I'll get you your poems and shit. Don't worry."

My heart's not in *The Free* anymore. Most of the crap I read just gets me down. But I told Deon I'd keep at it because I don't want to lose the cred that comes with the territory. Right now the Disciples of Vice are trying to prove themselves by getting me to print this lame-ass rap by one of their own, a kid named Felipe who can't rhyme for shit. I promised Cardo I'd run it so he'd shut up for once. Then, to appease the Bank Street Boys, who are "at war" with the Disciples, I've got to print this "essay" by one of theirs about how racist the criminal justice system is.

Whatever. At least Deon's happy. And Klein thinks we're "building something big" with *The Free* by giving fucked-up kids a voice or something. Not like anyone's listening, except other fucked-up kids. I start running that essay through the spell-checker, but I can't stay focused on it. I keep flicking back to Healy's face in that email from my lawyer. I've never seen a dead body before, and I can't make sense of this particular one. When Ms. Jomolca told me the cops were having trouble finding Healy, I was hoping he'd left the state, maybe gotten into that pickup truck and just disappeared. He has an uncle in Chicago. I remember him saying that once. Why would he run to that shooting gallery in Revere? Even when I knew him back in that shithole shelter, he wasn't into the hard stuff. Booze and pot, those were Healy's things. But heroin? It doesn't make sense.

The room gets quiet all of a sudden. It's because Barbie's stopped typing. The girl types like she's punishing her keyboard, like it's one of those dumbass banger wannabes she hates, some asshole that needs some sense smacked into him. Now she's looking at me like she just figured something out.

"What?" I ask her.

"You tell me, Ike."

I turn back to my laptop and that essay covered in red marks from the spell-checker. Right next to it is Healy's face, silent, blind.

Gone.

CHAPTER 41

It's colder than usual in the visitors' room on Saturday. They must be serious about saving on their heating bill, because that radiator isn't doing anything. It's radiating more cold if anything, like it has an attitude about it too. I'm nervous as hell over what I'm about to do, and when the bell rings and people start shuffling in, I change my mind. It's a dumb idea. Possibly my dumbest yet. Then my visitor comes in, hands stuffed into the pockets of his Carhartt jacket, eyes darting around the room, like he doesn't want to be seen. For the first time ever, I'm afraid of the man.

"That was a nice touch," he says when he sits down at my table. "Emailing the school principal."

"I didn't know how else to get in touch with you, Mr. Flannery. I wasn't sure that guy on the phone would pass you the message. He doesn't appreciate being called."

"Yeah, yeah, don't worry about it. So how you doing?"

"Not so great, Mr. Flannery. I heard about Pat."

"Yeah, I figured." Flannery rubs his papery white forehead with his freckled fingers. "It's a shame. It really is."

"My lawyer says it was an overdose."

"That's what they're saying."

"But Healy wasn't into drugs. Was he?"

Mr. Flannery shrugs.

"'Coz I remember how I had to pee into that cup for you. And Healy said he had to do the same thing. No druggies on the crew—I remember you saying that. No druggies, no thugs, no bangers."

"Yeah."

"So what happened?"

"You're asking me?"

I stare at him for as long as I can, trying to read something there, but I can't. He's not going to make this easy on me.

"I heard you got an extension on your sentence," he says. "That true?"

"How'd you hear about that?"

"I make it my business to hear about things. The hell's that about anyway? You get yourself a boyfriend in here? Some Latin lover boy you don't want to leave behind?"

Is he referring to Cardo? Does he know who my cellie is?

"It's complicated," I tell him.

Mr. Flannery chuckles. "Ain't it always. Well, look, you gonna be okay with that? With the extra year I mean? 'Coz you know it doesn't have to change anything."

"What do you mean?"

"I *mean*, you do your time, you can still come back, pick up where we left off. A year, thirty days, it doesn't matter. Nothing changes."

"Really?"

He meets my stare. "Sure. Just don't do anything stupid like get your GED in here. You play your cards right, you can get out of here and come straight back to the Voke, stay till you're twenty-one. Half the auto kids are in their twenties. I had a kid once who was twenty-five before the higher-ups figured it out." He laughs, real casual. But then he bites his lip and I realize his leg is bouncing up and down. He's as nervous as I am. And it's not just because he doesn't want to be seen here. "So what do you say?"

"How did you do it?" I ask him.

"Do what?"

He waits me out. He wants me to show my hand. He wants to know exactly how much I know. Of course I could pretend I don't know anything, just play dumb. A part of me wants to do that. Just forget what I know and go back to the way things were between us. If only I could get Healy's face out of my mind.

"Did you hold a gun to his head?" I ask. "Make him stick that needle in his own arm?"

Mr. Flannery closes his eyes for a second. His body has gone still, finally, and when he opens his eyes again, he looks like the whole world just shifted on him.

"Did he beg for his life?"

"What are you doing, Isaac?"

"He was your nephew."

"Second cousin."

"Is that how you justify it?"

"Jesus, kid, I thought you were smarter than this." His voice is low.

I match it. "It was never about protecting Healy, was it? It was about protecting you *from* Healy. That's why you asked me to take the rap. You knew Healy would never go down quiet."

He sneers. "Really? You put that together yourself, did you? Must be some kind of genius." He drops his voice to a sharp whisper. "Of course I had to protect myself. Who's gonna run the operation if I'm behind bars?"

"Your own flesh and blood?"

"You're the one that lost your nerve and ratted him out," Flannery says. "For chrissakes, Isaac, I put my trust in you. And what do you do? You roll over like a little pussy the second things get tough. What the hell did you think was gonna happen?"

He's right. I should have known. I can see that now. I can see a lot of things now. My eyes are wide open for the first time in my life.

Strange, I once believed in Mr. Flannery. It seems like a lifetime ago, back when he first took me onto his crew, bigged me up on account of how I passed that drug test, told me how mature and focused I was, how I was wise beyond my years. He seemed so smart to me then, like he had it all worked out. I never figured him for a murderer. A thief, sure. An ex-con. But not this. It was a clean operation. No violence. No guns. No druggies, no thugs, no bangers. That's what I thought. Because that's what he wanted me to think. I've got to hand it to him. He played me like a stolen car radio.

"So I guess I can't trust you after all," he says to me.

I know exactly what he means, so he can lose the cold stare. I know where I stand with him. And, yeah, I'm scared. Sure I am. But that's not all I am. Something inside of me has died, something vulnerable, the part of me that believed I was special to him, the part of me that turned this degenerate car thief, this murderer, this killer of his own damn family, into a father figure. Yeah, that's dead now. I was never special to him. I was useful. Now I'm a threat. And I know how he deals with threats.

"Sure you can trust me, Mr. Flannery," I tell him.

His eyes narrow. He's looking for my angle. He knows I'm not stupid enough to think I can bluff my way to safety, pretend I'm cool with the new plan of serving my sentence and returning to Donverse. He's right too. I've got something else in mind, something I stayed up all night cooking up. It's the reason my nerves are so jangled, the reason I can't stop bouncing my knee under the table.

"You sure about that?" he asks.

"I'm sure." I take a breath and do my best to calculate the wisdom of what I'm about to say next. But there's no reason. The whole world has just shifted on me too. "You can definitely trust me, Mr. Flannery. For ten thousand dollars."

"Excuse me?"

I look around at the nearby tables. "You really want me to speak up?"

Flannery leans forward. "What the hell do you need ten thousand dollars for?"

"It's probably best if we keep that on a need-to-know basis. But I can guarantee that I will not tell anyone about your involvement in stealing that car or murdering Pat Healy as long as you get me that money."

An icy smile spreads across Flannery's face. He leans back and slides his hands along the edge of the table, like he's making sure it's still solid. "You're *blackmailing* me? Is that what this is?"

"I'm pretty sure that's what they call it. Yeah."

"Mm-hmm." He arches his eyebrows. "You sure this is a road you want to go down? Because I don't think you do, kid."

"No, I've thought about it. And, yes, I do."

"How am I supposed to come up with ten thousand dollars?"

"How much did you get for that Escalade?"

Flannery laughs out loud. "Damn. The kid's grown a pair. What are they feeding you in here? Bulls' nuts?"

"No. Just the usual. Chicken, pork. Those little mini pizzas sometimes."

"Listen up, kid. We had a good thing going here. But you pull this shit on me, it does not end well for you."

I know I have to stay hard here, keep my game face on. I've just declared war on a guy who's not afraid to kill his own relatives, a guy who's connected enough to find out when someone's snitched.

"You have until Wednesday to get the money together," I tell him. "Come back then, and I'll tell you where to send it."

I stand up and walk away before any chickenshit thoughts get the best of me. When I glance over my shoulder, Flannery is still sitting there, running his hands along the edge of the table. He doesn't look amused anymore, the way he always does when something unexpected happens—like he's seen it all before, like nothing could ever surprise him. Because now, and possibly for the first time ever, a kid has surprised him for real.

CHAPTER 42

The next three days are hell. I know that if Flannery can come up with ten thousand dollars to buy my silence, he can come up with ten thousand dollars to have me killed. Even in juvie. Hell, there are guys at Haverland who'll do it just to up their cred before graduating to Walpers.

One day at lunch, Wayne starts making his way over to the geek table and I *know*—just know it in my gut—he's got a knife in his pants. Deon picks up on how nervous I am and starts asking me who the hell Wayne is. I've got my hands on the bench so I can get out quick in case Wayne comes at me.

"What's up, Isaac?" Wayne says. He's looking around, all nervous. "I don't know what you said to Barbie, man, but she's wicked pissed off about it. Keeps saying how you a traitor and shit 'coz of how you won't come back to group. But you know some of the guys, we been thinking maybe we need to cut you some slack. Things got really out of hand in there. It happens sometimes."

Okay, so he's not on the verge of knifing me, which is the good news. The bad news is that he's just as determined to get me back into group as Barbie is. These people are like junkies. Once they get a taste of your pain, they can't get enough.

I stand up and pull Wayne off to the side.

"Look, man," I say. "I'm real sorry about what happened. I never meant to hurt you or nothing."

"Naw, we're cool. It's just everybody's worried. Like we're responsible."

"No way, man," I tell him. "For real. That was all me. And I appreciate what you're saying. I do. I just . . . I got a lot on my plate. You know how it is, right?"

Wayne grunts. He might know how it is, but that doesn't mean he agrees with my way of dealing with it. He's a goner for group, buys the whole package. At least he's decent about it though. He gives me a quick fist bump, then lets me get back to the geeks.

When I sit back down, Deon waves his hand in front of his face.

"Man, you stink."

He's right. I'm sweating like crazy. I can feel it running down my sides.

"What you scared of? You owe that dude money or something?"

Wayne's already on the other side of the room, sitting at his usual table.

"Naw," I tell him. "I don't owe him nothing."

CHAPTER 43

On Wednesday, Flannery's a no-show in the visitors' room. Instead this other dude comes to see me. I don't recognize him—some middle-aged, fat white guy with a bushy gray mustache that looks like a rat's living on his face. He has a big brown envelope in his hand, and I'm thinking, *What an idiot. Don't bring the money here.* I have it all worked out with Cardo. The money's supposed to go to one of his associates in Saugus. Some guy at a pizza shop. I was planning to give Mr. Flannery the address when he showed up today.

"You Isaac?" the guy says.

"Did Flannery send you?"

He nods, keeps standing.

"Aren't you gonna sit?"

"Nah, I don't think so." He tosses the envelope across the table. It's light. Lighter than it should be.

"Aren't you gonna open it?" he asks.

"Here?"

"Go ahead. Open it."

I pull it under the table and peel back the two metal clasps. But when I reach in, there's no money inside. Instead, I pull out a stack of photographs, around twenty of them.

"What's this?"

My heart stops.

There's Janelle outside the middle school. Janelle walking home. Janelle at volleyball practice. Janelle walking down the street with some girl who must be Daniela. Janelle looking out her bedroom window. Janelle putting the trash in the dumpster out back.

They have every minute of every day covered. They have her on the playground at school. They even have her inside the lobby of our apartment building.

"I'm gonna need those back," the guy says.

I don't move, so the guy takes them out of my hands, stuffs them back into the envelope and reseals it.

"And I got a message from a mutual friend of ours," he says. "He wanted me to tell you, with Patrick there was no pain. With her, there will be."

CHAPTER 44

That night I stare good and hard at my bedsheets. There's a bottom one, fitted, and a top one, flat. But where would you hang them? The top bunk isn't high enough to dangle from. There's nothing sticking out of the ceiling. Would I have the balls to do it? I want to. It's the only way I can think of to guarantee Janelle's safety. *I'm* the threat to Mr. Flannery. Not her. Flannery's only using her to keep me quiet. And there's nothing quieter than dead.

I put my head under the pillow and hug it to my face, feel my breath disappear. It gets hot, tight. My head throbs. Everything goes black. Then the blackness prickles with colored lights. Starbursts and confetti. Something expands in my chest. Not air though. There's nothing going in. I hold on to this feeling for as long as I can, tasting death, teasing it. Can I do it? Can I hold on long enough?

There are angels in this world. Angels like Janelle. Miracles of goodness in this shitshow of evil. Only they're not here to protect us. We're supposed to protect them, keep them pure, keep them gold, keep that goodness alive. I squeeze the pillow tighter, feel the world closing in. I can do this, I think. I can protect her like I'm supposed to.

But my arms give out and I go on living.

Lying in those bedsheets, staring at those springs, drenching my pillow with useless tears. I can't even die right.

Maybe if I'm lucky I'll die in my sleep.

CHAPTER 45

The next day in the computer room I get an email from Janelle.

Hey Isaac. I hope you're holding up okay. Things are fine here I guess. Mom's still sober, but I don't know how much longer she has. Yesterday she dragged me to the supermarket because I swear to God she forgot how to buy food. All she did was get like a million two-liter bottles of ginger ale. Then she picked a fight with the checkout girl because she didn't have enough money to pay for it and she couldn't do the math to figure out how much to put back. Then she got all weird and started to apologize to the checkout girl. She even tried to hug her, and the girl was all, um, no thanks, you can go now. I swear, Isaac, it's like having a child around here. Seriously, it's easier babysitting Daniela's little brother. Sometimes I think Mom's better when she's drunk. At least then I don't feel sorry for her.

"Yo, Isaac." Deon slides his chair over to mine. "I need that shit from you, man."

"Yeah, I'm on it," I tell him.

I shoot Janelle a quick email telling her to hang on. Try to appreciate this phase while she can. I know our mom will be back to her drunk-ass self in no time, and Janelle won't be thinking it's better. Right after I hit Send, my inbox pings with a new email from someone named jas1959@gmail.com. I figure it's spam, but I open it anyway, because I can't break the habit.

Turns out it's not spam at all. It's a photo of Janelle leaving some apartment building I don't recognize. Alone. At night. Maybe Mrs. Rodriguez's after babysitting.

Jas1959 is not a name that means anything to me, but the meaning of the picture is clear enough. It's got to be from one of Mr. Flannery's guys, maybe the one who came to see me. She looks so innocent in the photograph, just minding her own business. She has no idea Flannery's on her tail. And I don't have the heart to tell her. It wouldn't do any good. There's nothing she can do about it.

"Why the hell you just sitting there staring into space?" Deon asks, but quietly so Klein won't hear. "I told you, man, I need that shit."

This gets Barbie's attention. She's sitting on the other side of Deon, snooping. "Aw, you know Ike," she says. "He's thinking those deep thoughts of his. Got to do it on his own too, 'coz none of us criminals smart enough to help him."

Actually these two, Deon and Barbie, are probably the smartest kids I know.

"Man, you got to snap out of it," Deon says. "You'll waste your life. You got to start thinking about what happens after all this. When you're back in the free."

"Aw, let him have it, Deon," Barbie says. "The boy doesn't have the nuts to stick it out in here."

"What do *you* know?" I ask her.

Barbie gets up and takes the empty seat next to me. Then she brings her lips close to my ear and whispers, "I know you're a pussy-ass liar can't face up to what you done. And what's been done to you."

I jerk away from her. "You don't know shit, Barbie. You have no idea what's going on right now."

"So fill me in, Ike. I'm all ears."

I turn to Deon, who finishes up what he's typing then faces me. "What is it *now*? You attack someone else in group? Add another year to your sentence?"

"You really want to know?" I ask him.

"Yeah, I want to know. But hurry up 'coz some of us have work to do, can't spend all day wondering what the hell is up with you."

When I don't answer, Barbie gets frustrated and IMs me:

—*Type it if you can't say it.*

Ah, the magic of the written word. Like I said, people write down all kinds of crazy shit they'd never say out loud. So why not me?

The only problem is, why should I trust these two? For all I know, they could be working for Flannery. I trusted *that* guy and look how it worked out. What is trust anyway? It's just another word for risk, another word for gambling on people you don't really know. If you can make it through life without trusting anyone, you're better off.

But there's one thing I do know about Barbie Santiago. Group is deadly serious to her. The fact that I'm on her team means something. As much as I hate to admit it, it means something to me now too.

"Go on," she murmurs out loud. "We got you."

So I start typing. I tell them everything. I don't spare the details. From Flannery ordering the theft of that Escalade all the way to him threatening my little sister. I put it all out there.

Deon huddles close to Barbie so he can read our IM over

her shoulder. When I get to the end, he gets on his own laptop, jumps onto our IM and types out:

—*Why don't you go to the cops with all this? Bust that guy once and for all?*

Barbie shakes her head, then types:

—*Because they in on it, right?*

I shrug. I can't be sure, but I have my suspicions about the police.

—*I knew it,* she types. —*I knew it when you told us that bullshit story about that guy hitting his head on a rock.*

—*That was the story Flannery told me to tell.*

—*Yeah, because he cleared it with the cops first, right?*

—*Maybe.*

—*What about your lawyer?* Deon types.

I shake my head.

—*You don't trust your own lawyer?* he types.

—*Somebody tipped off Flannery when I tried to snitch on Healy in court. Happened real fast too. Like, that very day. Only people in there were the judge, Ms. Jomolca, and my stupid lawyer. It doesn't take a genius to do the math.*

Deon shakes his head, then types, —*So you need protection from this dude and the cops and your own lawyer? Damn I thought I had some shit.*

—*Hey what about that ADA who was supposed to be getting you off?* This is from Little Anthony, who's all the way on the other side of the room.

I look up from my laptop and he waves at us.

—*You breathe one word of this Ant and I'm on you like stink on shit.*

—*Yeah, yeah. But what about that ADA? She seemed wicked into busting somebody else for that Sal Christaldi thing. Why you don't hit her up?*

Barbie types, —*The problem here is Ike's Bossman got eyes*

and ears everywhere. So we go to the ADA with this we don't know Bossman won't hear about it, right, Ike?

Barbie, completely getting it.

—*Yeah Ant,* I write. *So keep your mouth shut. For all I know Bossman's got eyes and ears at Haverland too.*

Nobody types anything for a while. Then Anthony writes —*Well, good luck with all that* and adds a little smiley face.

"Luck," I say. "Yeah, that's what I need. Like maybe a piano falls out of a building and lands on Flannery's head."

"That shit can be arranged," Deon says. "If you got the cash."

"If I had that kind of cash, you think I'd be in here?"

Deon stares at his laptop where our IM has gone cold. "Sorry I can't help you," he says. "You think of anything, though, you let me know."

Barbie doesn't move. She's still staring at her laptop, her beautiful eyes narrowing to slits.

"What?" I ask her.

"Nothing," she says.

So much for the power of the written word.

THE NEXT DAY, BARBIE shows up to the computer room with a vicious grin on her face. I wonder if this is what she looked like out in the free when she was about to stir some shit up. She practically sprints to the laptop across the table from me and starts IM-ing.

—*Can you get a message to your sister? One that Bossman won't know about?*

—*I can email her.*

—*That'll work. She babysitting today? Over at the Rodriguezes' place?*

—*Yeah. Why? You know them?*

—*Yeah, Ike. All Hispanics know each other.* She shakes her

head. —*Get me their address and find out if they got a back door, a fire exit or something. Can you do that?*

—*I guess so.*

—*Don't be guessing, Ike. You in this or not?*

—*In what?*

—*In the master plan, buddy. What you think I'm talking about?*

—*What's the plan?*

—*The plan is your sister goes to the Rodriguez house to babysit just like usual, right? If Bossman watching her, he won't think anything's different. Just a typical day. But then instead of leaving like usual, she goes out the back door or the fire escape or whatever and that's where my cousins Mateo and ChiChi come in.*

—*Who are they?*

—*I told you, they're my cousins. They gonna pick your sister up in their van, take her to my tía's house. I already talked to my tía. She's good with it, got an extra bed downstairs, no problem. She'll keep her safe. Meanwhile, you're gonna call that ADA, tell her what Bossman been up to so she can arrest that MF then put your sister some place safe.*

—*You mean like witness protection?*

—*Yeah, but they got stuff that's special for kids, like out of state or something. Just show her them photos Bossman sending you so she knows your sister's in danger.*

—*Then what?*

—*I don't know. Wait for the trial I guess.*

—*Will my sister be safe?*

—*Yeah I told you, they got stuff that's special for kids. A friend of mine knows a guy who did it.*

—*You really think it'll work?*

—*That's up to you, Ike. My cousins gonna be there if I tell them to be. And my tía's solid. Your sister'll be safe with my people. I can promise you that. But you got to deliver on the ADA. She ain't gonna listen to me.*

Across the room, Little Ant is waving at us and giving us the thumbs-up. He loves this plan, thinks it's ingenious.

I have my doubts. I'm not saying it's a *bad* plan. Barbie's done her homework, worked her connections. She's a damn queen for doing it too, pulling favors for my sake and Janelle's. I've never had anyone do that kind of thing for me. And her plan *is* pretty solid. Smart, sneaky. But I've made a lot of plans in my life. Doesn't matter how great they seem at first. Shit has a way of going down. It's the stuff you don't see coming, the details you never thought of.

"Yo, Deon," I say. Then I show him the IM with Barbie.

Barbie rolls her eyes, but she's proud of her work, happy to show it off.

"What do you think?" I ask him.

"You sure you can get that ADA on board?"

Barbie leans across the table and whispers, "Oh come on, Deon. Boy's got a lead on a homicide. Guy killing his own nephew."

"Second cousin," I say. "And keep your voice down."

"Whatever," Barbie says. "This shit's got to get her attention. Especially if you already on her radar, right?"

"Yeah," Deon says. "But now you going up against someone big, someone connected. This guy seems like bad news."

"I know," I whisper. "But I don't think he's got the ADA in his pocket."

"How do you know?" Deon asks.

"She never liked my story, never believed it. She wanted me to turn on Healy. That doesn't sound like someone in Flannery's pocket."

Barbie IMs, —*Don't pussy out on me now, Ike. This plan is tight. We taking Bossman down!*

I wish I had Barbie's confidence. It's my sister's life I'm playing with here. I can't take chances. I want guarantees.

But at the end of the day, what choice do I have? I can't leave Janelle on her own out there with Flannery and his goons. Besides, now that Little Ant, Barbie, and Deon know what's going down, I can't be one hundred percent sure this won't find its way back to Flannery. Things have a way of leaking. Just by inviting these guys into my problems, I may have put Janelle at risk.

So I email Janelle, ask her about the fire escape situation at the Rodriguez house.

She's at study hall, so she gets back to me right away and we switch to IM.

—*Of course they have a fire escape*, she writes. —*Why?*

Then I break it all down for her. It comes out in a rush, full of typos; I'm typing the way Barbie does, fast and hard, about how Mr. Flannery's watching her, and how the only way out is for her to slip out the fire escape at the Rodriguez house and take a ride with two bangers from Sol Dominicano. When I finish, there's a long pause.

—*Are you kidding me?* She finally writes back. —*If Mrs. Rodriguez finds out there are gangbangers driving up to her house, she will kill me. For real.*

—*Then you've got to do it real sneaky, Janelle. Just slip out the back when she's not looking. Trust me, there's no other way. Flannery's watching.*

—*And this guy's your teacher?*

She's still playing catch-up, still trying to connect those dots. Things were already bad in her life, and I've just made them worse. But I don't have time to spell it all out for her; the bad news is chasing us down at a sprint.

—*He's a killer, Janelle. He killed his own cousin. The kid was eighteen years old. We've got to move on this. We've got to move now. Today.*

The IM goes cold for a minute, then she types:

—*Didn't you always say I should keep my distance from gang-bangers? Didn't you tell me to watch out for Daniela's brother? Since when are you making friends with Sol D?*

—*Things move fast, Janelle. You've got to trust me on this.*

Barbie, reading over my shoulder, takes over my laptop.

—*Hi Janelle. My name's Barbie Santiago and you don't know me but I'm the one setting this thing up. Your brother, Ike, all he wants to do is protect you. But he can't do that from inside, so that's where I come in. Sisters gotta look out for each other, right? So don't be worrying about Mateo and Chichi. They tight. I ask them for something, they on it. They the good kind of gangbanger, responsible and shit. They'll get you to my tía's safe and sound. You got my word on that.*

—*Isaac?* Janelle writes.

—*I'm here Janelle. Barbie's right. New game, new rules. We've got a plan here. All you have to do is go to the Rodriguez house after school, just like normal.*

—*And that guy'll be watching me?*

—*He's not going to hurt you. It wouldn't make sense now. He's only doing this to threaten me. Just head to the Rodriguez house like it's a normal day. You can do this, Janelle. I know you can.*

—*I'm scared.*

—*I know. But this is how we fix things. This is us getting out. Just like we always planned. I've got leverage now. I know things about Flannery that I can use and I'm gonna use them. I'm gonna get us out from under all of this. Will you trust me, Janelle?*

Again, she doesn't answer right away, but this time it's all the answer I need. Why should Janelle trust me? All I've ever done is let her down, put her in harm's way. If I were Janelle, I wouldn't trust me either. Trust is a loser's game. But what choice does she have?

CHAPTER 46

Right after computer class I get in line for the pay phone. It's almost 5 P.M. and there are nine guys in front of me and six guys behind. One of the guys behind me is Cecil Boone. He's leaning against the wall, staring straight ahead. At nothing. Nobody looks at him. Nobody's that stupid. When he sees me walking up to him, he gets his game face on.

"I loved your poem," I tell him.

It takes him a second, but I think he recognizes me. "Yeah?" he says real low.

"Best one I read. It'll be in the next issue of *The Free*. You've got real talent."

Lie, lie, and lie. I couldn't even understand Boone's poem. It's about someone who walked out on him. Her name's Charlene, but you can't tell if she's his girlfriend or his mother. There were much better poems, but now I'll *have* to print it.

Boone falls for it though. He nods his big fat head like I'm just telling him something he already knows.

"So I was wondering," I say. "I hate to do this, but I need a favor."

"Kind of favor?"

"It's just that I'm in a wicked big rush here. I've got to get this lady on the phone before she leaves the office and it's almost five already."

Boone looks down the line of guys in front of us. "The hell they taking so long for?"

"I know, right? It's just . . . It's my sister. She's in trouble. I don't mean trouble with the law. She's not like that. She's a good kid. An A-student. But somebody's after her and—"

"Somebody's after your sister?"

"Yeah. To get to me. She's only thirteen. And if I don't make this call in time . . ."

Boone looks down the line of guys again, then steps out and waves for me to follow him. "Save my place," he tells the kid right behind him.

The kid's on it, doesn't even need to be asked. The kid will fight off a tiger to save Boone's place.

Boone strolls up to the front of the line with me at his side. All the guys look annoyed at first, ready to say something, then wise up. The guy on the phone is speaking Spanish quietly but real intense. Boone reaches his giant hand (the thing is the size of a foot) straight across the guy's face and pushes down the receiver.

"Time's up," he says.

The guy looks pissed, but he figures out the situation quickly and hands the phone to Boone.

"All yours," Boone says, handing it straight over to me.

"I owe you."

"Nah, we're good." He walks back to his place in line.

CHAPTER 47

In person, Jill Levy is not what I expect. She's blond, gorgeous, in her thirties. When I spoke to her on the phone, I got the distinct impression she didn't believe what I was telling her. After all, she explained, Patrick Healy was found dead of an overdose, with a needle sticking out of his arm, a stone's throw from a well-known shooting gallery. She had to agree with the cops: That didn't look like murder. But when I asked her if there were any other track marks on Healy's body, she got real quiet.

In the end, I think it made about as much sense to her as it did to me that a kid who never used heroin before would decide to shoot himself up alone, in an alley, in the freezing cold. Kids are stupid. But they're not that stupid.

She pressed me for more details over the phone, but I held back. It was going to be a tit-for-tat situation between us. She didn't like that idea so much, but she agreed to show. And now here she is, in a conference room at Haverland, the same one where I lied to those cops about Healy's mug shot being on that laptop.

"Okay, Isaac," she says. She opens her briefcase and takes out a big yellow notebook and an expensive-looking black pen. "I'm listening."

"Patrick Healy was afraid of dying," I tell her. "Specifically, he was afraid of dying in prison. That's why I took the rap for him on the Sal Christaldi thing."

She nods, jotting down notes. "Okay. Before we get to Salvatore Christaldi, let's just focus on Patrick Healy for a minute. You're in here and Healy's out there, but somehow you know he was murdered?"

"Yes."

"And the name of his murderer?"

"Is the same individual who ordered Healy and me to steal Sal Christaldi's Escalade."

"*Ordered* it?"

"Yeah. It was a steal-to-order job. The buyer specifically wanted an Escalade, specifically of that year. Healy and I cased it for three weeks. I don't know all the details, but I'm pretty sure it went straight onto a container ship the night we boosted it. I can tell you where we dropped it off. But I don't know any of their names."

"Yeah, you're not so great at remembering names, are you?"

"Look, I'm trying to help you now. I know I should have come forward sooner, but—"

She waves her hand to shut me up. "I don't suppose you have proof for any of this?" She's doubtful, but I have come prepared. I slide her a printout of that email from jas1959@gmail.com, the one with Janelle's picture on it.

"That's my sister," I explain. "They emailed me that so I'd know they're watching her. They showed me a whole bunch of other pictures before that too. Janelle at school, Janelle at her friend's house, babysitting. They've got her covered. If I say anything, they'll kill her. If they know I'm talking to you, they'll kill her."

"*They* being?"

"This particular individual and his associates."

"And the individual's name?"

"Yeah, I'll tell you his name. I'll tell you everything I can. But first I need some protection."

She looks up from her pad. "We can keep you safe in here," she says.

I laugh. "Yeah right. Anyway, I'm not talking about my own protection. I'm talking about my sister. Once I tell you his name, it's gonna take some time to play out, right? You'll arrest him. There'll be a trial. I need her somewhere safe while all of that happens. I cannot have her out in the open for even one second."

"Okay, so you want police protection—"

"No! Not the police. The police are in on it."

She stares at me, hard.

"At least I think they are," I say.

"You *think*?"

"Look, no one in here believed that story about how I stole that Escalade all by myself, then pushed it into a pond. So the way I see it, either the cops are dumber than a bunch of juvenile delinquents, or they're in on it. And how about how I punched Sal Christaldi and he landed on that rock? They laughed at me in here. They had all kinds of questions. The cops never asked me nothing."

"Mm-hmmm."

"You never believed that story either, right?"

She doesn't answer.

"Look," I tell her. "All I'm saying is, I don't want the police protecting Janelle."

"Isaac, can I ask you a question?"

"What?"

"Why isn't your lawyer here?"

"I didn't call him."

"Why not?"

"What do I need him for?"

"It's just that normally when someone's attempting to strike a deal with the DA's office, they bring their lawyer along," she says.

"Maybe I don't like my lawyer so much."

"Is he in on it too? Ian Slater. Is he part of this scam?"

"I didn't say that."

"But you think that, right? The cops, your own lawyer? They're all part of this?"

"You think I'm paranoid."

"I'm just trying to get all the facts, Isaac."

"I'm giving you the facts."

"You're giving me a pretty sizable conspiracy theory, Isaac, and, look, I'll be honest with you. I have never liked this case. You're right about that. I never believed your story. The whole thing stank from day one, as far as I'm concerned. But I'm not seeing anything here that rises to the level of evidence." She looks down at the photograph of Janelle.

"Fine. Forget about the cops and my stupid lawyer. I'm not here to give you them anyway. I'm here to give you the guy in charge. Maybe he'll give you the cops and my lawyer. All I'm saying is the cops can't be the ones protecting Janelle. You have to do better than that."

Ms. Levy sighs. "What are you saying? You want her in witness protection?"

"Yeah, something like that. But where she can go to school. Someplace far away. Like out of state. My friend says you have something like that. Maybe Canada or California?"

"Canada's not a state, Isaac. It's a foreign country."

"Fine. Just someplace away from here."

She sizes me up.

"When I tell you who this guy is, Ms. Levy, you'll see. He's not just anybody. He's an upstanding member of the

community. At least people think he is. When word of this
gets out, it's gonna be big."

She chews on her pen for a while. "There's this farm in
Vermont," she says. "We stowed someone there last year.
They take in troubled kids."

"Janelle's not troubled. I don't want her in some halfway
house."

"I meant kids *in* trouble. Usually from their parents. Last
year we sent a kid there for about a month while his mother
testified against his father. He liked it so much, he didn't want
to leave. After his father went to prison, his mother moved
up there to work on the farm. I think they're still there."

"A farm? So what, she'll be milking cows and stuff?"

She cracks a brief smile. "It's an experimental school.
And, yes, it's also a working farm. It's a pretty special place
actually. And it's free, run by a couple of retired profes-
sors. Old money. Eccentrics. They only take kids in trouble.
That's their mission." She pulls out her phone, taps a few
buttons, shows me a photograph of some white kid with his
face pressed up against a cow's butt. Another picture shows
an old white couple and a group of kids posing in front of
a red barn. One of the girls—around sixteen, dark skin, big
teeth—looks a little bit like Janelle.

I feel something like hope stirring inside of me, which
makes me scared. "And you could get her there now? Like
tonight?"

"I could get her there by *tomorrow*. Maybe the next day. I'd
need to make some calls."

I take her phone and scroll through the pictures. It's not
what I was hoping for. I was picturing some nice, rich family
with a big house, driving Janelle to a fancy private school.
Maybe a lawyer and a doctor whose kids have already grown
up. I definitely wasn't thinking of a *farm*. But after looking

at the pictures, I can almost see Janelle there. Milking cows, breathing all that fresh air. Maybe when the trial's over and Flannery's in jail, she could even visit me at Haverland once in a while. Maybe get one of those old folks to take her on a field trip.

"I assume your parents are on board with all of this?" Ms. Levy asks as I hand the phone back.

"What?"

"How old is Janelle?"

"Thirteen."

"Right. So we'll need parental consent. Mother? Father? I assume they're in the picture? One of them?"

"Um . . . Yeah . . . it's just that . . . our mother . . . she's . . . well . . . You don't know my mother, Ms. Levy. She's not like a normal mother."

"What do you mean?"

"She's just not, okay?"

"What about your father?"

"He's . . . um . . . I don't know where he is."

"Can you track him down?"

"No."

"Why not?"

"Because I don't know *who* he is."

"I see."

"Can't we just skip that part?"

"Which part?"

"The part where you tell our mother?"

"Isaac, I can't just whisk an underage girl off to Vermont without parental consent."

"But—"

"That's not how it works."

"But she's in danger."

"Does your mother agree with this assessment?"

"My mother doesn't know anything about this."

Ms. Levy arches an eyebrow. "Then maybe it's time to bring her up to speed."

"Are you kidding me? She'll never agree to this. She'll never let Janelle go. She's—"

"Look, Isaac," she interrupts gently. "I want to help you. I do. If you tell me the name of the person who's responsible for the death of Patrick Healy, we'll arrest him. Your sister won't be in any danger then."

"He's having her followed!" I grab the printout with Janelle's photo on it and hold it up to her face. "You see that name? Jas1959? That's not him. That's someone else. Someone who works for him. Right now he's probably reporting back to my boss that Janelle's missing. She's in hiding right now, waiting for you to come get her."

Ms. Levy shakes her head. "Isaac, why would you do that? Why would you assume I'd 'come get her'? I never made that kind of promise to you. When we spoke on the phone, I didn't have any idea you were going to ask me to place a *child* in protective custody. I told you I would come and listen to your story. That's it. I am not in the habit of kidnapping thirteen-year-old girls."

"You said you'd help me."

She stares at me, like I'm the one who screwed up here, like I'm the one who's not delivering the goods. But that's bullshit. I'm delivering Tom friggin' Flannery on a silver platter, and she's got nothing. I stare right back at her, right through her stupid pretty face and her shiny blond hair, straightened stiff the way Janelle does it sometimes. She's already white. Why does she need to look even whiter?

"I'm sorry," she says finally. "I'm sorry I can't be more help."

"*Can't?* You mean *won't.*"

"My hands are tied, Isaac."

This lady is just like everyone else. That social worker from DCF who gave my mother "a second chance," the principal of Worthrop High with his "zero tolerance" policy on bullying. Judge Hayes with his extra year of "rehabilitation." Sorry kid, rules are rules. We can't go bending them for your sake. Or your sister's.

I get up and head to the door.

"Isaac, wait! Tell me his name."

I turn around. She's so hungry for Flannery's name she's practically glowing. She smells a story. Maybe she even smells fame, the chance to take down some dirty cops, a dirty lawyer, get her name in all the papers. Janelle's safety means nothing to her. She's only thinking about herself. What a surprise.

"We'll do everything we can to protect you," she says.

I laugh. I laugh in her pretty blond face.

CHAPTER 48

It was a good plan. It should have worked. Between Barbie and me, we had all the details covered. And there Janelle sits, at Barbie's tía's house, waiting for Jill Levy to whisk her off to Vermont.

Only Jill Levy isn't coming. Jill Levy is stuck, just like I'm stuck, and the person sticking us both is the same person who's been sticking me my whole life. Will it ever change?

Janelle can't stay with Barbie's tía forever. Eventually, Mr. Flannery will get suspicious. If he isn't already. Who's to say he doesn't have a snoop in the DA's office? Maybe he already knows I'm trying to sell him out.

Above me, Cardo whistles in his sleep. He sleeps like a baby now, running himself down with all those push-ups and sit-ups, leaving our cell stinking of sweat. Cardo's lucky. Things are simple for him. Shitty, but simple. A judge and a jury will decide his fate. Until then, the Disciples are calling the shots. They own him, just like Karen West owns me and Janelle.

What kind of world puts people like her in charge of people like us? In a sane world, she wouldn't qualify to raise a goldfish.

I know I'm no saint. I've done some pretty awful things in my time. But I'm better than my mother. From the minute

Janelle came into my life, I've loved her more than my mother ever did. I've fed her, bought her clothes, *stolen* her clothes, taken care of her when she was sick. I've gotten her into private school, forged signatures, run away with her. Every single thing I've done—the smart and the stupid—has been for Janelle. And what has Karen West done? Neglected her. Hit her. Sold her. But because Janelle spent nine months inside of her, Karen West gets to call the shots.

Cardo's whistling sings out soft and high. Somewhere on the unit, a guy mutters in his sleep. On the cement floor, that red light throbs. Then it's quiet and still, and something comes to me.

Something perfect and terrible.

CHAPTER 49

She's sober. Cleaned up. Almost pretty. She's washed and bleached her hair, put on a bit of makeup. Not too much. If you squint, you could almost see a normal mother there.

"How you doing, Isaac?" she says.

It sounds like an apology. For what though? For whatever she can remember?

She collapses onto the bench. She smells clean, like shampoo, instead of her usual vanilla perfume.

"What's going on?" she says. The look of total confusion reminds me how much she doesn't know. I'm not sure she ever knew when I was supposed to be getting out of juvie. She was so drunk when I was sentenced, it barely registered. According to Janelle, she kept asking where I was that first night.

Sobriety always clears her mind, but it doesn't fix her memory. She's lucky like that. She doesn't need a box to store bad memories in. The booze washes them all away. Hell, that's probably what the booze is for.

"Janelle's been gone for three days," she says. "Is she mad at me? We haven't even been fighting. I've been so nice to her."

Of course. She's not confused about me or my sentence. She's confused because she's alone. The one thing she can't stand.

"Janelle's fine," I tell her. "She's safe."

"But where is she?"

"Mom, I need you to sign this." I slide a piece of paper across the table. She squints as she tries to read it. She needs glasses but she won't get them.

"It's a consent form," I tell her.

"What for?"

"You need to sign it."

She holds it at arm's length and tries reading it sideways. "Vermont?" she says.

"It's like a boarding school. It's for her own protection."

"From what?"

"From a lot of things."

She reads some more, then puts the paper down and rubs her forehead. "Is she mad at me?"

"Mom, I need you to focus. You really have to sign that. It's important."

"I'm not sending Janelle to *boarding* school. She's twelve years old. She needs her mother."

"She's thirteen. And what she needs is to go there."

Her lips are cracked and dry, her skin pale, even through the makeup. Rehab has cleaned her up but it's also taken something out of her. She looks raw, vulnerable.

"I know things have been hard," she says, "but they're better now. We all just need to settle down and—hey, when are you coming home? I thought you'd be out by now."

"You're not listening."

"Is that lawyer helping you? Because I have *never* liked him. He's a snoot. Taking our money, then . . ." She leaves it at that.

Mr. Slater never took any money from us. He was assigned by the state or the county or whoever assigns these things.

I push the paper back to her and put my felt-tip pen on top of it. "Just sign it."

She pushes it back. "I am not sending my daughter to boarding school. Jesus, Isaac, why are you giving me such a hard time? If you knew what I've been through. I've got that social worker hassling me, the landlord. I've got two people from Janelle's school bothering me. And some priest keeps coming around asking about you and Janelle getting baptized. What the hell is that about? We're not Catholic. Janelle's been out of school for three days. And the principal's blaming *me*."

"Sign that piece of paper and it's all taken care of. They'll talk to the principal and DCF. You won't have to worry about anything."

"I am not sending Janelle to boarding school. Are you crazy or something? What makes you think I'd do something like that?"

It came to me in a flash last night: probably the best plan I ever came up with. Now I have to fight just to keep it alive. My throat dries up. All my instincts tell me to run, to bury it, to stuff it back down in that box where it belongs. But this is my last chance, my final card. If I don't play it, it's game over.

"Because if you don't sign that consent form, I'll tell DCF what happened in Ashland."

My mother looks confused. She shakes her head like she's clearing out space to make room for what I just said. Then something flickers across her face. A memory. *The* memory. The booze hasn't erased everything, after all. It's been there all along, and now it's out in the open. It won't go back in the box. It's too big. It's bigger than the room, bigger than all rooms. How did it ever fit in that box? How did we ever do anything but tremble in its shadow?

I push the paper and pen back to her. "Sign it, or I'll tell

them what you did to her. And how I let you." I take a deep
breath, then bring my eyes up to hers. I know I have to look
at her. She has to know I'm serious, that I'm not afraid to tell
them everything. "It's you they'll punish. They'll take us away
from you for good. You'll never see either one of us again."

"I can't be alone," she whispers.

"You won't be," I tell her. "Not if you sign that. I get out of
here in one year."

"A *year?*"

I pick up the pen and hold it up for her. "If you don't
sign, you lose both of us forever. If you do sign, you only lose
Janelle."

I can see her working through it. Underneath the hurt
and the demented belief that she's the victim here, she's
sizing up the situation, looking for the best possible out-
come. For her. She hates being played like this. She'll spend
weeks, months, *years* stewing about the wrong I'm doing
her. She'll haul it out for the rest of my life.

"You don't know what it's like, Isaac. You don't have any
idea how hard it is. Raising two kids on your own. No help
from anyone. Not even my own mother. You know she dis-
owned me soon as she met your father. You think it's easy
when your whole family thinks you're trash?"

"Sign it."

She tries to wait me out, stare me down. She even digs out
that cold stare that pinned me to the couch in Ashland. But
I don't flinch. I'm beyond that now. The part of me that was
capable of being scared like that is dead. She can look at me
however she wants. The only thing that matters is Janelle.

"You don't have any idea the sacrifices I've made for you,"
she says.

She rips the pen out of my hand, finds the *X* on the page,
and stabs out her signature.

I turn the paper over. "You need to sign there too."

"You think you're so smart," she says. "You're just a kid. Just a dumb kid. You don't know what it's like out there. What people can be. What they're capable of."

When I don't answer her, she finds the X and signs a second time.

I take the paper and stand up.

"So stop judging me, Isaac! You wait! You wait till you have two kids counting on you. No money coming in, no man around. No family. Neighbors think you're trash. Your friends turn their backs. You think I've had it easy? You think I haven't made sacrifices for you?"

I put my back to her and walk away.

I can hear her getting to her feet.

"You come back here, you little shit!" she shouts.

"Ma'am, that's enough," a guard warns.

I don't turn around to watch the guard manhandling her to the door, but I can hear it just fine.

"Don't you put your back to me! I'm your mother, goddamn it. Look at me!"

She's my mother all right, but she's not my problem anymore. She's that guard's problem now, and I'm confident the guard can handle her. I'm done handling her.

When it comes to Karen West, Isaac West is done.

CHAPTER 50

I think it truly surprises Jill Levy when I deliver the signed consent form to her in that conference room the next day. She takes her time examining my mother's signature.

"It's legit," I tell her. "Go ahead and call her if you want. She signed it right in front of me."

"The location in Vermont is secret," she tells me. "Your mother won't be able to visit."

"That's not a problem."

"You're sure?"

"Yeah," I tell her. "I'm sure."

I hand her a piece of paper with the address of Barbie's tía written on it. "That's where Janelle's staying. She's ready to go now."

Ms. Levy bites her lip but nods. "My assistant will pick her up tomorrow."

"Can't it be today?"

"I need some time to arrange things. She'll come by tomorrow morning. If you want to write to each other, you can use my address. My assistant will forward your letters." She hands me her card, then puts the consent form and Janelle's address into her briefcase and shuts it with a sharp snap. "Now, the name of the person who killed Patrick Healy."

"You can't move on that until Janelle's safe."

She brushes a strand of that pretty blond hair behind one ear and stares me dead in the eye. "You have my word that she'll be safe."

"Actually, I want a picture of Janelle once she's there on the farm. But don't email it. Bring it to me in person. Then I'll give you the name."

She sighs in frustration. "You're really getting on my nerves, Isaac."

"I know," I tell her. "But trust me, you're gonna love this name."

"I better."

THE NEXT DAY JILL Levy shows up with a photograph of Janelle in a kitchen somewhere in Vermont, presumably, with two old white people standing on either side of her. She looks nervous, out of place. The kitchen is big, with a gigantic old-fashioned stove and a big red kettle on it. I wish I could speak to the old couple, get to know them, make sure they're the kind of people who can take care of Janelle the way she deserves. They *look* nice, for whatever that's worth. Rugged. Like farmers, I guess.

"They're good people," Ms. Levy says. She can see how nervous I am. I'm actually trembling. "Your sister will be fine."

"Can I keep this?"

She nods. "The name, Isaac?"

"Tom Flannery," I tell her. "He's the head of the auto department at Donverse Vocational."

"Donverse? Isn't that where you were enrolled? Were you a student of his?"

"We all are."

Her eyes widen. "What do you mean?"

"His whole crew," I tell her. "We're all his students."

Her face lights up like she just won the lottery.

I NEVER GET TO see Tom Flannery's face when he gets the bad news. He sings like a bird, though, when they take him in. I like to think of him as one of those dirty seagulls down Revere Beach way, the ones that flock around the garbage cans and hassle you for your hot dog. I'm pretty sure Mr. Flannery sees himself a different way. He takes down a dozen cops with him, plus my stupid lawyer, which must make Jill Levy's day. Apparently keeping your "mouth shut" does not apply to Tom Flannery.

He'll have an interesting time at Walpers, rubbing elbows with the guys he took down. Then again, dirty cops aren't going to do so well at Walpers either.

The story gets front-page treatment in all the local papers and on wickednews.com, which I read in the computer room. The comments are wild. People are actually shocked that a criminal enterprise of this scope was operating right under their noses—in a suburban high school, no less. I find this hilarious. Who did they think was stealing all those cars? Joy riders? Homeless people? Out-of-staters? Auto theft is an art, as Mr. Flannery once said. What better place to practice it than a vocational school with an auto program run by an ex-con. Maybe next time do a better job hiring teachers. Maybe do a criminal background check, for example.

Deon is in heaven. He's writing an exposé on the corrupt Donverse police force. It's not just GTA. There are rumors of drugs and prostitution too. "Pure gold," in Deon's words. He's emailing back and forth with Jill Levy. I'm not sure how much actual information she's feeding him, but she told him he has "chutzpah," which apparently is Jewish for *balls*.

A FEW DAYS LATER I'm in the cafeteria with my tray and Cecil Boone waves me over to his table with the Bank Street Boys. Since you do not say no to Cecile Boone or Bank Street, I head on over.

"Everyone loved your poem," I tell him. "Got a lot of great feedback." I make sure this is loud enough for his friends to hear.

Cecil beams. "I got another one for you," he says. "Can't sleep no more. I'm writing all the time. Whyn't you sit down. We got space for you."

Bank Street inviting me to sit with them? Believe you me, I am tempted. Having Cecil Boone and the Bank Street Boys catching your back is not something you take lightly. But then I catch a glimpse of Deon and the boys at the geek table. "Man, I would love to join you," I tell him, "hear all about your new poem and everything, but I . . . um . . . I got some newsletter business to discuss with Deon and the geeks. You know how it is. Keeps us hella busy. All kinds of folks submitting to us now."

"You gonna have room for mine?"

"There's always room for you, Cecil."

I put my back to Cecil and the Bank Street Boys. I know there won't be any drama. Truth be told, because of my position on *The Free*—not to mention the fact that I helped put away a bunch of cops—I could probably sit anywhere I want to. But I'm sticking with the geeks because they stuck by me.

CHAPTER 51

About three weeks later, Janelle comes to visit me. She has this new winter coat that looks mad expensive, with zippers and Velcro everywhere. Her hair is in neat braids in a spiral around her head. When we hug, she smells different, like a farm I guess. It reminds me of that time we snuck into the Topsfield Fair and had to hide behind the horse stable until it was safe to come out.

"So, you're a farm girl now."

I don't tell her that she *smells* like a farm. I'm so happy to see her, she could smell like a sewer and I'd be okay with it. She looks healthy and happy. That's what matters.

"I can't wait for you to come," she says. "Edson and Jo Jo are dying to meet you. They're waiting outside."

Edson and Jo Jo are the old couple who run the farm. He's a poet (an actually *published* poet), and she's a horticulturalist, whatever that means.

"Maybe later," I tell her. "So you still like it there? They have showers and everything?"

"Oh God, I smell like a goat, don't I?" She sniffs her coat. "I don't even notice it anymore. It's from milking them, I guess."

"Goats?"

"Yup. Every morning. That's one of my jobs."

"So, they've got you working."

"Yeah, but we take classes too. And they are super strict about our schoolwork. They're, like, *scholars*, you know. And then there's these tests we have to take for the state or something 'coz of being a charter school. Then on Saturday morning, we have the market, and I get to run the cash register. You would not *believe* what people will pay for eggs, Isaac. And goat's milk. We sell raw goat's milk. I didn't know milk was cooked. Did you know that? Did you know that the milk you drink is cooked?"

I have never known anything about milk, except that there's plain and chocolate.

"You're gonna love it there, Isaac."

"Is Mom still calling you?"

"Ugh. I wish she didn't have their number. She *was* calling every day, but I told her I'd only talk to her once a week. She's drinking again."

I knew it wouldn't take long. She held out for almost a month, which is a record for her. Stupidly, I allowed myself to hope that it would be different this time. But why would it be? Some people can't change. If you keep waiting around for it, you're the jerk, not them.

"I do worry about her sometimes," Janelle says.

"Don't. Worry about yourself. Mom is not your problem."

"Yeah, I know, but what's gonna happen to her?"

This is a conversation I've been dreading. Janelle is under the impression that I'm coming to live on the farm as soon as my sentence is up. I never told her I was, but I never told her I wasn't, either. I had to make sure she settled in there. I didn't want her getting ideas about coming home once I get out of Haverland.

"Isaac? What aren't you telling me?" Her hands fly up to her nose. "Oh my God. You're not coming, are you?"

"Janelle, look—"

"But why? I told them all about how you studied cars. And Jo Jo says that could be really useful on the farm. I know it sounds weird and everything, but it's not, Isaac. We go walking in the woods sometimes. And there's a lake for swimming in the summer. And you'll like the other kids. I know it's the middle of nowhere, but . . ." She searches my face. "You promised her, didn't you? You promised you'd come home. That's why she let me go." She closes her eyes. "I'm so stupid. Why else would she let me go? You bargained with her. I can't believe you did that, Isaac."

"I did what I had to do."

"But I don't want to be away from you."

"You're better off being away from me, Janelle. Look where I am."

"So?"

"I'm a criminal, Janelle."

"Don't say that."

"But it's true. I wasn't in the wrong place at the wrong time, either. I stole that car."

"You think I don't know that? I'm not stupid, Isaac. And I don't care. You're my brother."

Just then, a little kid from the next table toddles over and trips on Janelle's shoe. Janelle bends over to help him, but his mother, some girl around seventeen, scoops him up, plops him on her lap, then slumps over the table with her cheek in her hand, bored. The guy she's visiting, around seventeen, antsy, keeps talking at her like she's his lifeline. He doesn't care how bored she is; he's going to keep on talking until the guards take her away.

"There's something you never understood," Janelle tells me.

"What?"

"I never blamed you," she says. "Sometimes I think you blame yourself for what happened, but I never did."

"Janelle—"

"I know you don't want to talk about it. Believe me, I don't either. But you need to know that it wasn't your fault."

I feel like I've been punched. And like she's broken a promise.

"It was her, not you," she says.

It was an unspoken promise. I'm not even sure how we made it. But it was understood that we'd never talk about Ashland. It wasn't a story we could tell or a secret we could share. It was like a crack in the universe. Talking about it meant living with it, and neither of us—no matter what we've been through—is damaged enough to live with something like that. But before I know it, my head's in Janelle's lap and I'm sobbing. Big, wet, noisy sobs with tears spilling everywhere.

"I'm sorry," I tell her. "I'm so sorry, Janelle." I'm crying so hard it shuts everyone up. I don't care. After a few minutes, I sit up and wipe my face.

"I've been crying a lot too," Janelle whispers to me. "Jo Jo says there's a well of tears inside all of us, and we have to bring up the water whenever we can." She laughs. "She says some pretty weird stuff sometimes. But she's really smart. Hey, that reminds me, I brought something." She pulls a small plastic bottle out of her coat pocket. When a guard gives her a dirty look, she shakes it for him. "Holy water," she says.

The guard looks like he's about to come over for a second look, then changes his mind.

"I know it doesn't matter now," she tells me. "But I wanted it anyway. For you and me. But not Mom. It's not actually from a priest. It's just from Jo Jo. She said a prayer over it from a book. She said as long as we believe it's holy, that's all that matters. So let's just say we believe, okay?"

"Okay."

"And it's just for us."

"Just for us."

"And not Mom."

"Not Mom."

She opens the bottle, dabs some water on her fingertip. "I'm not sure what to do actually, so . . ." She rubs it on my forehead. When she gives me the bottle I do the same to her. Then we press our foreheads together and close our eyes.

I'm hoping something important will happen, like a weight lifting or a cloud parting. Or maybe even the heat suddenly coming on in that freezing-cold visitors' room. But all that happens is our foreheads get slippery, and when we pull apart, the water feels cold.

Still, something about it feels right. It's something only we will ever know about. A secret we don't have to lock up in a box. This secret can run free whenever we need it. When we're feeling lonely. When we're missing each other. It belongs to us.

And not our mother.

"I'm good now," Janelle whispers. "I'm safe."

It's all I've ever wanted. To hear those words and to believe them. No matter what else happens, no matter how long I have to stay at Haverland or what I have to go home to, if Janelle's safe, then everything's okay.

She takes a pair of thick wool mittens out of her coat pocket and wipes the water off of our foreheads. "So don't worry," she says. Then she smiles with those square teeth I love so much. "It's about you now."

CHAPTER 52

We've got this new girl in group. Black, fifteen, a real hard case. She's been in listening mode for a week, and now it's time to read her crime story. When she comes in, she's hugging her notebook to her chest like it's going to protect her from something. She should know better than that.

"Are you ready, Desreen?" Dr. Horton asks her.

Desreen swallows.

"It's okay to be nervous," Javier says.

"Yeah, you be a warrior later," Barbie adds. "Right now you just give those words to us and we take care of them for you. Ain't that right, Isaac?"

Barbie turns to me, and when she smiles that crooked smile, her gold tooth flashes. But I don't hate it anymore. There is nothing about Barbie Santiago that I hate. How could I, after the way she stepped up for me? She put it all on the line just to help me and Janelle. Barbie Santiago is my miracle. Maybe someday I can be hers.

"That's right," I say. "They're just words, Desreen. Just words on a page."

Desreen soaks it up, trying to find the strength to open that notebook. I'm not sure she ever finds it. I think she just figures she has to get this part over with. Whatever she's hiding, it won't stay hidden forever. Things have a way of spilling out into the open whether you want them to or not.

I guess it all started 'coz I wanted these earrings.

She's a thief like me, a shoplifter. She worked with her friend, Tandi, boosting things from the mall. Risky stuff. The mall has cameras everywhere. As she tells her story, I'm right there with her. When she knocks that shop girl to the ground, when she aims that gun at her face, we're all there, nodding, looking her in the eye, willing her to keep going, to tell us everything and hold nothing back. Her voice is so quiet, we have to lean in to hear.

Tandi was telling me to just shoot the bitch, but I didn't want to do that, so I smashed her in the face with the gun instead. I went backhand and forehand and split her lip. There was blood everywhere. Then Tandi tries to grab the gun out my hand and that's when it goes off.

While she's reading, I can feel myself lifting up and away. But it's not like that time I went apeshit. That was me trying to escape my own head. This time it's more like I'm seeing things for what they really are but with an extra dimension or something. And these facts Desreen is sharing, these details about this or that, they're just things that happened, things that she did. But once she brings them in here, they become something else. A story.

Then I realize that Ashland is like that too. There are the terrible things that happened that day—the things I did and the things I didn't do. And then there's the *story* of Ashland, the one I shared with these people. Sharing it means it's not a secret anymore. And the thing about a secret is that it has more power than you. The more you hide it, the more powerful it gets. Now that I've shared it, something feels different. I'm not free of it or anything. I know Ashland will always be with me. But it's not bigger than me anymore. I'm bigger than it.

Then I feel something I've never felt before. I don't even have a word for it. It's like I've been living under a shadow my whole life, and now the shadow is gone. I can see things, possibilities, futures I've never imagined. Maybe I *will* go live on that farm with Janelle. Maybe there's some way to make that happen. Why the hell not? If I can be an editor on a juvie newsletter, why not that? And why not Barbie too? Maybe she'll come with me. Maybe she'll win her court case and we'll both be farmers and live in Vermont.

Stupid, right? The odds of Barbie Santiago going to Vermont with me are about as long as me winning the lottery. I'm no fool. I know most of the kids at Haverland—hell, most of the kids in this room—are bound to wind up in prison. Or dead. But those are just facts, like the ones Desreen is sharing now. And facts aren't everything. They're just raw material. The things you can't change because they already happened. What matters now is the story. And how you tell it. How much you lie. How much you tell the truth. What you include, what you leave out. Who you tell it to, and how they take it in.

"Um . . ." Desreen says. "That's all I wrote." She closes her notebook and sits back in her chair.

She may think she has something behind her with that story, but already we're sharpening our claws.

"So, Desreen," Barbie says. "You want to tell us 'bout how that gun goes off on its own, with no finger on the trigger? Or you just forgetting something?"

"Yeah," Wayne says. "I was wondering 'bout that myself."

Desreen's face shuts down. She looks to Dr. Horton, but he's not going to save her. Well, he might, but not in the way she wants.

Barbie makes a gun with her hand. "'Coz I'm thinkin' if I gotta role-play this and I got a gun in my hand, where the hell my trigger finger at?"

Desreen gives Barbie a look of death, which only makes Barbie smile. She's one tough bird, squaring up against Barbie Santiago like that. I have to give her credit. But no way is she scaring Barbie off. Barbie is fearless. She feeds off looks like the one Desreen's throwing at her. She'll keep clawing at Desreen's bullshit story about a gun "accidentally" going off until she draws blood. Then she'll claw some more. That's how it works in the orange-rug room. You bleed and bleed, but you never bleed out.

"Desreen," I say. "How much time you got in here?"

"One year."

"Good. 'Coz sometimes it takes a few tries before the truth finds its way out of that notebook."

"Yeah, listen to Ike," Barbie says. "He knows all about that."

The others laugh.

Not Desreen though. She's on her way to hell. And she thinks Barbie is leading the way. But she's wrong there. If anyone's going to get the truth out of her, it's me. Thief to thief. Liar to liar. And I have plenty of time to get it too. Eleven months to be exact. So I can get in deep with Desreen, cut through the bullshit, straight into that gaping hole at the center of her heart, that darkness so black she can't even see it. I can lead the way, all right. But I won't be alone. I'll have Riley, Sandra, Javier, Wayne, and Barbie Santiago backing me up. No matter what Desreen thinks of us now (and I can see she's working up a big hate), we're the only ones who can guide her on this journey she's about to take.

To hell and back.

Because we know the way.

Ask Barbie Santiago

You got problems? I got answers.

Dear Barbie:

This girl I was getting with for like two, three weeks got herself pregnant and now she's asking me for child support. But I never signed up for none of this. It was like more of a casual relationship if you know what I mean and anyway I think she was trying to get pregnant cause she told me she was on them implants. So what do I do about this?

Signed,
Daddy-No

Dear Daddy-No:

First off ain't no girl out there capable of getting her own self pregnant without there's some dude helping out. Second, why you having relations without using your own protection? It ain't just pregnancy gonna get you. So that's your own fault. And finally you can't claim she trap you into daddyhood when you be boning her of your own free will, so you got to stand up now and take care of that baby. You don't do right by that child you be dying a little bit every day and taking that innocent life down with you. You a man or what? Stand up, brother, or I be coming after you.

—Barbie Santiago

Dear Barbie:

My cell mate has stankbreath. I don't want to hurt her feelings but what am I supposed to do?

Signed,
Can't Breathe

Dear Can't Breathe:

According to the Internet bad breath is usually caused by gastrointestinal type situations, so you're best off just telling her straight up. That way she can start eating right and stop making everybody sick all the time, 'coz believe me you ain't the only one noticed that stink. Trust me on this one, girlfriend, you have a chat with her, you be doing her and everyone else a favor.

—Barbie Santiago

Dear Barbie:

I once tried to order a hit on my own mother. It didn't work out in the end, and now I have to deal with her. I feel guilty about it but also she's a wicked shitty mother. Any advice?

Signed,
Too Broke to Kill

Dear Broke:

The world be putting you into all kinds of impossible situations where what seems wrong is right and vice versa. But there be good in everyone. Even in your mother who maybe deserved to have that hit put on her. There are no angels in this world. But we do our best. If that's good enough for the God that made us it should be good enough for us too. So focus on the good in you 'coz it be shining out for all to see. I know I see it.

Peace out.
—Barbie Santiago.

Got a question for Barbie?

Stick it in that box by the water glasses. She'll get to it soon as she can.

The Free

Editor in Chief
Deon Wilson

Poems & Shit Editor
Isaac West

Editor at Large
Stanley Huang

Supervisor
Theo Klein

AUTHOR'S NOTE

When I began researching Isaac's story, I encountered kids who'd been "jumped" into gangs as children, kids who'd been sold into prostitution by their own parents, kids who'd been bumped from broken home to broken home, never finding anything like the kind of stability, nurturing, and unconditional love that most kids take for granted. In short, I discovered kids who, even before their eighteenth birthdays, had already endured lives of epic struggle. I wanted to write about their humanity, their stolen childhoods, and their dogged spirit of survival.

I also wanted to explore the surprising, and often ignored, flip side of the criminal life—the potent sense of camaraderie that comes with gang membership, the entrepreneurialism of the small-time thief, the ad hoc friendships and on-the-spot problem solving among kids for whom so many choices are literally life or death. For these kids, the world doesn't stitch itself together to catch them before they fall, like it does for the luckier among us. For these kids it takes extraordinary character just to get by. It's in their honor that I created Isaac West.

ACKNOWLEDGMENTS

Many thanks to Daniel Ehrenhaft, my editor at Soho Teen, who believed in this book from the beginning and without whose brilliant contributions and tireless support this book would not have seen the light of day. Thanks also to Sandy Smith, epic copy editor who understands the dark art of the comma better than I ever will, to Rachel Kowal for holding my hand through the entire editing process with indulgence and patience, and to Bronwen Hruska for her vision and encouragement—not to mention the Lambrusco!

I am deeply indebted to my agent Jill Grinberg who stuck by me with insightful criticism and tireless support through many drafts, and went so far beyond the call of duty that I'm not sure the term agent even covers it. Thanks also to her brilliant team, especially Cheryl Pientka, Kirsten Wolf, Katelyn Detweiler, and Denise St. Pierre.

Thanks also to Scott Westerfeld and Justine Larbalestier for reading an early draft and for always being generous with their wisdom and expertise. Thanks to Karen Gormley for her expertise in criminal justice. Any errors are mine not hers.

To Andrew Woffinden, my partner in crime and all things, thank you for being my confidence when my confidence was draining.

Thank you to my brother, Mark McLaughlin, for teaching me what unconditional love is at a very early age, to my mother, Carol McLaughlin, for believing in me through every iteration of an often chaotic artistic life. And finally, to my father, Tom McLaughlin, thank you for teaching me how to live with grace and empathy and for being the inspiration for Isaac West.